The COLOR of LIFE

The COLOR of LIFE

By
Dennis Vebert

I HOPE THIS BOOK ADDS A LITTLE COLOR IN YOUR LIFE.

**Sometime... the work you do,
is not seen by the ones
that you want to see it the most.
T. Dalton**

I dedicated this book to my beautiful wife for showing me all of the splendor in the world.

BOOK COVER AND ALL ART WORKS IN THE BOOK BY
DENNIS VEBERT
The book cover is called "Florida Forgotten"

Library of Congress Cataloging-in-Publication Data

ISBN 978-0-9842497-1-8

Book Design & Printing By
Creative Printing Services, Inc.
St. Cloud, Florida USA

Printed in the United States of America

First Edition

1 2 3 4 5 6 7 8 9 10

Chapter I

"It is my enormous honor to include this formable work of art of the true way Florida looked before the huge growth in our great state took away a good deal of our majestic scenery," spoke the Honorable Governor Gerald P. Roberts, a second term strong-minded Republican governor of the great state of Florida.

Along with the governor's personal secretary were about a half dozen on- lookers that attend this kind of event on a regular basis to indulge in the free food and drink or whatever handouts that are given for the occasion.

A whisk of cool fragrant air brushed the hair on the back of my neck that came from the ornamental tan wicker fan above my head, while a newspaper reporter moved across the room to set up his camera for the photo shoot.

"Sir, could you move just a smidge bit closer to Mr. Dalton?" he said.

"Yes, yes that's much better, thank you," the reporter said looking into the lens of his camera and focusing in on the governor and his guest.

"This magnificent painting by Timothy Dalton has captured the true essence of Old Florida," said the praise-worthy Governor while the news reporter was photographing him shaking my hand for a publicity shot.

Governor Roberts was a middle-aged favorably dressed person that thought he was more than he was. His coal black dyed hair along with the girdle that he wore made him look younger than he was. The political time in Florida was a time of unrest but Gerald P. Roberts was in his last term of office and was just doing projects that were popular to the general public. He was a well-liked politician, but people that knew him well, knew he was like numerous politicians that did most of their shenanigans in the back rooms instead out in the open.

Normally a very long winded person when it came to public speeches, he had no intension of taking too much

time for this occasion because he didn't sense this event was important enough for one of his typical sermon-like dialogues. Also there weren't enough of the right people to hear a good old fashion *...how great I am* speech. Besides after all it was a holiday weekend, and the Honorable Roberts had more important plans, spending the day out on his luxury yacht with his private secretary.

"Governor, it's time for your next appointment and you know how you hate to be late for your appointment," said the eye-catching secretary with a strong southern accent and a wink in her eye.

"You are a very talented artist," the reporter from the Tallahassee Star said, after the Governor walked away to mingle with the few more important guests that actually showed up.

"No, just lucky," I replied.

I always found it hard to accept a compliment for my paintings, thinking people were being kind or just making small talk. Whatever the case may be, it just made me uncomfortable. After all, I have heard great complements before, but talk was cheap and cheap talk didn't buy paintings.

"No sir, you are truly a first-rate artist, "said the reporter putting away his camera.

"Maybe you would allow me to do a full story about you some day. You know... where you are from and your schooling and how you got started painting the beautiful landscapes that you do so well."

"I'm afraid my life would not make for very interesting reading," I said.

"Perhaps, but when I latch onto an interesting story, I know how to present the story in a way that the public will enjoy it," the reporter said, shaking my hand again.

I was hesitant in committing to the reporter permission for him to do a story on me because I have had stories about me before and the person writing the story got everything wrong.

"If I could be assured that you got all the information about me correct, I might let you do it."

The reporter said, "If I wrote a story about you, I will show it to you first. Then if you didn't like it... well... it just wouldn't get printed, how is that?"

"I guess I could live with that."

The reception was modest, only a handful of dignitaries were on hand, compared to some of the more distinguished and elaborate events that Governor Roberts arranged. This function was in honor of a landscape image that I painted some six months earlier, and was chosen from about fifty five paintings submitted by other artists throughout the state.... that best portrayed the way old Florida looked in it's glory days. The painting was a representation of a typical swamp scene, with a cerulean blue sky and many stately burnt umber cypress trees, along with a good deal of slate gray Spanish moss hanging on the branches and with a number of egrets by the waters edge. The twenty-four inch by thirty-six inch painting was to be stationed in the great hall of the Governor's mansion in Tallahassee and came with an award of two thousand dollars not including the price of the painting of three thousand dollars.

I was making a modest living painting Florida landscapes on a full time basis for about five years up to now. Over the years I had my share of artistic rejection and I had to crawl up the ladder of the art world culture one rung at a time. The art world was quick to pass judgment on my work at first because I was poor and couldn't afford to enter art contests, where people can see your work... because I did not have the money to pay the entrance fee. Without a backer to promote your work so you can get the kind of recognition in the artsy-fartsy world you needed, you don't succeed very fast. I was very stubborn and didn't want to conform to what people wanted me to paint. I painted for the affluent class of people, for awhile... paintings they didn't appreciate and didn't really want or need, but the money was good and what I made from them I used to buy more paints and canvas. Now I have found a certain edge. An edge of a individual style that people recognized and wanted to see what I painted.

I now traveled throughout the state painting images of Florida landscapes that I thought people would like to hang in their homes. At times I wondered what the next subject would be that I could make interesting. After all how many ways can you paint a palm tree or a swamp but it was all the little things that I saw in a particular location. What colors would make it an attention grabbing painting and what details would appeal to the public. I just studied the lay of the land and some how I was able to capture what I saw on canvas. I didn't think I was the best artist by far but I also wasn't the worst either and if I felt that I would hang the painting in my house, well... it was good enough to sell.

I was so proud and humble to have my painting chosen, I rubbed my lucky silver dollar, and as I looked at the painting one last time before I departed the prestigious hall, my past came rushing back to me and to where the story all began. A good memory is fine, but the ability to forget is the true test of greatness and at this time I was far from being great.

Chapter 2

It was an exceptionally hot time of year in the summer of 1930 in sun baked Collier County Florida. The United States was in a frightful mess, with what is now known as the Great Depression. Most of the working class population was out of work and the rich were not rich anymore. Just months earlier in late 1929 the stock market crashed. Banks failed and many businesses closed. Very wealthy bankers and stock market brokers were jumping out of windows on Wall Street and taking their lives because they lost everything they had. There were others that had all their money tied up in the stocks and bonds... one day they were rich beyond their dreams and the next day they were totally bankrupt. Nobody was immune to the economic moment at that time, the Dalton family included.

The 30's were a time when the depression caused by the wall street crash caused the world to undergo a fundamental change in lifestyles. and part of the change was from the new radical politics.

It was a time of much unrest in Europe. A man by the name of Adolph Hitler was starting to make big changes on the political scene in Germany with his Nazism. People were being persecuted for their religious beliefs and were being forced from their businesses and eventually their homes too. Russia had their political turmoil too. The Czar was removed from power, his whole family was murdered and the government was taken over by a group called Communists. In Italy the challenge to the government was from Fascism, another radical group.

There were enormous dust storms in the heartland of America due to the lack of rain for several months. Gail force winds blew across the plains and stripped the land of it's vital top soil. Nothing was left but a sandy soil build up some ten feet high in spots, covering the few crops that the farmers tried to grow and also made food a short supply throughout the entire country. Several of the black dust storms were three miles wide and thousands of feet high and darkened the sky for days on end and made it almost impossible to go outside. Farmers had to stretch ropes from the barn to the house and to any other out buildings so that if they were caught outside when the wind started to blow they weren't going to be carried away. The black dust searched it's way into the smallest cracks and many people died from the dust in their lungs and from starvation. Seeing no end to the tragedy, people packed up everything they could salvage on whatever dilapidated trucks or automobiles and left their foreclosed farms and migrated to the West Coast looking for work and a new life only to be met by a negative response. Seen as outcasts they were forced to take refuge in migrant work camps. They worked for very little money and being forced to pay most of miserable wages for the high prices for food and rent where they lived, to the company store.

Out of work people in the large cities... which included entire families, stood for hours in long soup lines just to get something to eat. Although prices were very low on most goods, the fact that people didn't have any money still made it hard to get by.

The government was taking control of many banks

trying to stop the run on the banks by the public trying to withdraw what little money they had before the bank could close. Legislation was being passed to put the fourteen million out of work population back to work on projects such as the T. V. A., Tennessee Valley Authority. It was the governments line of attack by using the unemployed workers to build dams, roads and bridges but with so many people out of work the over abundance of workers was constantly present. Being poor was just a way of life.

In Collier County Florida most people never had much of the wealth as the rest of the country, so we didn't know what we lost since we never had it in the first place. The native population made a customary living fishing or catering to the few tourists that came to the local vicinity trying to get away from their problems. Even back then, people from the north realized the benefit of the laid-back comfort and the pleasant climate of the Deep South to try to kick-start their life again. Of course, at that time I was extremely young and I thought that life as I saw it was good. That is, I was happy... at least up to a point.

Daily showers washed over the land cleansing the

tropical landscape cooling the temperature a couple of degrees and lowering the heavy humidity to a more comfortable range. The heavy moisture in the air is somewhat hard to get used to if you were not a native Floridian. Small lizards basked in the sun, occasionally trying to break up the sporadic flight of the wily dragonfly. Impressive tropical aromatic blooming wild jasmine vines helped to cover up the unpleasant odor of the backwater cove where we lived. Whooping cranes and grotesque storks wading at waters edge made ripples and breaking up their reflection in the water while searching for the infrequent meal of small silver fish.

Three small rooms with a partial rusted screened in porch described the bleached white clapboard shack, the place that impressed me the most when I was a very young boy. The shanty sat on an out parcel of land several hundred feet from the backwater run off that ran out to the bay and eventually to the gulf. We were surrounded by thousands of small islands that splattered the landscape out to the gulf, some no bigger than large sand dunes.

The small structure was found abandoned when the crusty old black man that had squatted there about a year before was bitten by a white belly, other wise known as a water moccasin snake. He most likely had no friends to speak of and was too far from town to be able to get help. With that kind of snakebite he must have suffered excruciating pain and eventually he died. The locals discovered the man's bloated disfigured body, that must have been rotting for at least two weeks. In this stifling heat and with all the swamp rats taking turns at him... he must have been a frightful sight. They rolled the body onto a tarp and dragged his body to the nearby woods, dug a deep hole, threw in a bag of lime over him and then covered him over. After that the property was left abandoned again because people said it wasn't fit to live in because it smelled so bad. My Pa claimed the property that sat empty for about a year, and after a misfortune came to us nearly six months earlier. By then the smell had faded enough so that the shack was usable again.

Weathered oilcloth with a bold orange and white daisy print covered all the windows making the rooms rather dark when pulled closed. One wall opposite the one with a window was wall-papered with old news print with the head lines that told about the great stock market crash of 1929. The floor was constructed with weathered cypress uneven planks that creaked with a unusual sound when we walked on it, and the walls were constructed with the same type of boards and were painted to some extent a dingy off gray. The rusty tin roof made interesting music when rain drops played on it, giving us something more to listen to besides the general sound of the rain. The furniture that was abandoned with the shack had rotted and to replace it we accepted furniture that were handout donations given to us when the cabin we lived in the grove burned down in a lighting storm and destroyed everything that we had.

My clothes and what few toys I had were hand me

down from the congregation of the Southern Baptist Church at the east end of town, from people that had not much more then we did. With all this if truth were told, we did not want anybody to feel sorry for us because we were very proud people and only accepted help from anybody when there was no other way. I have to say again... it truly was at a time in my life when I was very happy. I had recently turned seven... a month earlier and I thought that now I was as grown up as I was ever going to be. A small child always believes what an adult tells them, and my Ma and Pa helped assure me of the fact that I was a grown up by always calling me their big grown up boy. I was raised with a certain amount of freedom and was considered an equal member in our small close knit family.

As I look back, my appearance was of a skinny little white boy with fine wooly unruly strawberry red hair and a multitude of freckles that almost lock together to disguise a skin with a tan over a light completed body. My Ma always kidded me about my large curious brown eyes. My Pa gave me the nick name of freckle face. I enjoyed running about in bib-overalls and walking in the sand without any shoes so I could feel the cool sand between my toes. The only drawback for being short for my age was that I had to bend my head back to look up to almost everybody that I talked to, and that I had to scrunch all the way forward in my chair just to reach the table. I did take advantage of my size by being able to reach the ground without too much trouble or to be able to crawl under or hide in things that taller people couldn't do.

It was a fun and special time in my life... a time that was spent in swimming, running and hunting through the cabbage palms behind our home, and fishing with my Ma and Pa on our small wooden white dinghy out on the Gulf. Or just walking near the edge of the water collecting shells with holes in them so that I could make wind chimes that made whimsical sounds when the wind caught them. It was a time of learning, like the time when my Pa found a bees nest in a hollowed out Gum tree and he showed me how to collect the honey by using a smoke stick to move the bees away so we could move in and get the sweet golden liquid candy. A treat well worth learning how to do when you wanted something sweet to eat.

"Timmy go fetch the gear ready, we have to go fishin

today," Pa said in his high nasal pitched voice.

"Ma needs sumpun to put on the table and we have to see what else we kin get that we kin sell," he continued as he leaned back in his chair after he finished his grits.

"It's time we made a trip up to Buzzard and get some supplies."

"I'll have everything ready by the time you finish drinking your chickaree," I said enjoying the responsibility that Pa gave me.

I just finished a big hot bowl of grits, gravy and a pan biscuit for breakfast the typical meal that my Ma made for me almost every day.

My mother moved to the wash basin with the dirty dishes chimed in and said, "Thank God for dirty dishes, they have a tale to tell. While others may go hungry, we're all eating well."

I think I heard her say that little ditty every time she did up the dishes.

" Don't forget to take some oranges to eat and a jug of water, ya might be on the Gulf fer a long time," she went on to say.

My sweet mother looked old for her young age of twenty-five but I thought she was the most beautiful woman in the world or at least in my world. She never complained about anything and I realize today that she sacrificed a lot. The only two dresses that she had looked alike, they went down to her ankles and had tight sleeves with a high neck collar, but they were forever clean. Her beautiful long golden-brown hair was always pulled to the back, braided, and tied with a strand of brightly colored ribbon. Ma was a petite person only five feet tall with unbelievable butter soft pale skin and had to be careful not to burn in the tropical sun. I guess that I take after my mother in that sense, where as Pa had rough tanned skin from working out in the sun so much. Mama had a light sweet voice, kind-of-like what I would imagine an angel would sound like. Every once in a while I could hear her singing a little folk song when she thought nobody was around. She was quite shy and didn't think her voice was very pretty. Among her other wonderful traits, she was an educated person that could read and write along with add and subtract numbers. My Ma loved to read and would read everything that she could, labels on food containers, the bible, flyers that she would pick up in town and on occasion she would find an old book discarded in the trash by a tourist. My Pa and me were quite fond of setting around a bon fire on cool evenings and listening to my mother reciting short poems that she memorized from a poem book that she once found. She tried to teach me to read and write when she could get me to sit still long enough but I didn‘t realize at that time how important it was.

Chapter 3

"A-a-h boy, were hit as bad as what we heered it twas?" asked a old timer wiping hot salt sweat from his head while wasting the afternoon sitting on the white cement steps of the First Bank of Henderson Creek.

The veteran soldier just home from the war in Europe, the war that they said was the war to end all wars replied, "Worse sir, worse than whatever ya could have heered."

The boy, still in a hot Army uniform and carrying a large grimy duffle-bag across his shoulder, was one of many young boys home from the bloodshed in Europe at the end of World War I. He was stopping at the bank to cash his last pitifully small military check from his discharge from the U. S. Army. He was like many boys out of the service at that time wandering the land looking for that elusive job and trying to put his life back together.

"Is there any work to be had around cheer, sir?" the young man inquired.

"Nope," said the colorful resident with a toothless grin.

The elderly man scratched his bald head and spit a slug of tobacco juice over his shoulder said, "But if'n ya need sumpum to eat and a place to rest, ya can go to the Southern Baptist Church out east of town. I reconin they are giving out meals to soldier boys that don't have any money or a place to stay."

"I haven't had good home cooked meal for I don't know how long, and I sure would be mighty thankful for a place that I could git some rest before I git back on the road," the boy said setting his duffle-bag down on a step.

"Mind watchin this cheer duffle bag fer me whilest I go chash my government check?"

"Sure thin sonny, anythin fer the U. S. Government Army."

After cashing his check and getting directions to the church the boy arrived just in time for the once a day hot meal that was prepared for the wayward Army boys.

"Would ya-all like seconds?" said the young girl as she looked intently at the dashing soldier boy.

"I sure would, ahh... ahh... what's yur name gal?"

"Sands."

The girl hesitated for a moment and said, "Grace Sands, I mean."

"That is sure a purty name to go along wit such a purty gal."

Putting another large helping of food on the boys plate and not being able to take her eyes off him she said, "What's yur name? Are ya a general?"

He chuckled with a mouth full of food. "Na... ma'am, jest a lowly Private. Private Hector Dalton... I mean just Hector Dalton."

The soldier paused to take another huge bite and said in a shy way, "Just Hec... that's what everybody's called me most all my life... and I would be happy if'n ya would call me Hec."

"Sure nough, Hec."

The young man went and sat at a table so that he could eat proper and Grace finished what she was doing and then went to sit beside the boy. She was drawn to his good looks and shy demeanor. One thing Grace wasn't when she was young, was shy. She wanted to know more about Hector and she was bound to do just that.

"Are ya hitched Hec?" She was figuring that she might as well get the big one out in the open so that she would know if she was wasting her time or not.

Hector put down his fork and said, "Nope... ya surly like to git right down to business, don't ya gal?"

"I don't want this to go no farther if'n ya was, now the next question, do ya have any gal-friends?"

"Gal are ya gonna let me get this good food down? No I don't have any gals, ya got to member I just got out of the Army."

"Have ya got a place to stay tonight, Hec?"

Now that's a good question, and no ma'am... I was just figgerin on sleepen out by the swamp tonight."

"Well most of the house-holds in town that have extra room are putting up veteran soldiers fer a few days or at least til they kin git on the road again. Maybe I kin find ya a place to stay fer a night or two, if'n ya want me to?"

Most of the residents that were putting up service men were at the church in a meeting. Grace mingled from one person to another and found all she asked were already filled up for the rest of the week. In concern for

Hector, the girl decided to take him home and asked her father if he could stay there for a few days, knowing that they had extra room because of the terrible losses in their family some time back.

"Pa, this cheer is Hector Dalton, Private Hector Dalton, of the United States Army. He's just got home from fighting in the war over in Europe. Now poor Hec ain't got no place to stay fer the night and after all he done fer our country and us... don't ya thin we could put him up fer a few nights? Hu, Pa? Hu?"

"Hawdy boy. My name's Sands, Marion Sands... most people jest call me "Mar" and ya already know my youngun. Gal go show Hec to a room and make him comfortable. We'll go outside later and sit a spell on the porch and ya kin tell me all bout the war over thar."

Ma baked some molasses cookies and when they were done baking they all went out on the porch where Mr. Sands asked, "Where where ya stationed, boy?'

"Mostly in France, sir."

"Mar... boy... jest call me Mar," he insisted.

Hector was just finished with his fourth cookie and said, "Grace these are the best cookies that I ever et, do ya think I could possibly have another?"

"Give the boy another one of those sweet thangs, gal, so he can go on wit the story. Did ya git to see a lot of sights in France?"

"No sir, I mean Mar, mostly what I saw was a lot of mud holes that we crawled in and out of. It was a terrible hell hole, with a lot of dead Germans and some mighty fine horses that were kilt from all of the shellin and bombin that we did on them poor souls. But it was either them of us, ya know. I seen boys right next to me wit legs blown away and others wit not much left of their heads. Sir, I mean Mar... I'd rather not talk much more bout the war if'n ya don't mind."

Mr. Sands on a whole was a matter-of-fact, hard working self-respecting God-fearing individual and saw a lot of the same traits in my Pa.

It must have been love at first sight with my mother, because she spent all of her time with my Pa for the next few days and hardly let him out of her sight. She walked him all around town showing Pa all of the interesting sights, but really what she had in the back of her mind... she was just showing Pa off to the townsfolk. She also took him fishing to emphasize how good she was with a fishing pole, and then cooked the fish they caught to show him how good a cook she was. Oh, and of course she had to bake Pa a sweet tator pie and more of those great molasses cookies to get on his sweet side. By then Pa was well under the amazing charm of my Ma and couldn't live without her. Mr. Sands was quite impressed with Pa too, and took a liking to him right off, because he didn't object to him when Pa asked Mr. Sands for his daughter's hand in marriage.

It was a stunning day for a wedding, not a cloud in the sky and no hint of rain despite the fact that it was in the heart of the rainy season. But chances are if it was going to rain it would most likely be in the evening and the ceremony would be long over with by then.

Pa was fitted out in brown tweed coat over a new pair of bib over-alls with his army shoes shined the best that they could be. Ma even put a small blue wild flower in his coat button-hole. My Ma was in a white cotton dress that she made, that went down to the ground and had long sleeves and a high collar with wild yellow field daisies on her shoulder. Her father gave her a bone carved pin of a woman's head that belonged to her mother and she pinned it to her dress. Even Mr. Sands got dressed in his very best work clothes and Ma made him a new palm frond hat to wear on the occasion.

The wedding party was small without any of the towns' people in attendance. The preacher had his wife stand in as a witness and the wedding party all gathered in the front room of the small country church. When the preacher asked my Pa if he takes my Ma as his wife, he... I was told, turned a pale off-white and as he said "I do," almost passed out. With the short service over, Pa kissed my Mother and they moved to go outside.

On the day of the wedding, an automobile drove up and parked outside the front door of the church and out of the vehicle stepped a middle-aged good looking man. He was clean-shaven and didn't look like he did very much heavy labor by the way he was dressed. He neither smoked nor chewed tobacco. His shoes were shiny and he wore a flat straw hat that was cocked back from his forehead. A few minutes later he was in the process of setting up a large wooden camera on a extended tri-pod. Then the traveling photographer started taking pictures of the front of the quaint country church where the small ceremony was taking place when my parents got hitched.

As they were coming out of the front door the man introduced himself to the wedding party and said that he was on assignment from a book company in New York City.

"I am taking photos of the state of Florida, the colorful buildings, landscapes and the interesting people that I meet on my way through Florida for a book that might get published. My publisher is sending people all from beginning to end of the United States and doing the same thing as I am doing. The publisher is wanting to put together a set of books all about each state... the land... folk lore... customs and architecture in the union, and I got Florida for an assignment. If I may take a picture of the happy married couple, I will give you two copies when I get them developed."

"Well sir, I can't see what it would hurt, sids it might be sumpun nice to hold on to," my Pa told the man.

I never saw a photo of my Pa in his Army uniform and I never asked him what it was like to be in a war and he never volunteered to tell me. Ma said he was very shy and so handsome in his soldier uniform that she couldn't take her eyes off him. I do remember seeing a picture of my parents when they got hitched but I don't know where that photo is today.

"Ya say they are hiring men to work on a new road that is going from Naples to Miami across what they call Alligator Alley?" Pa was asking another boy just out of the Army and getting ready to go farther south Florida for a job.

"That's what I heered, but ya better not be a'waitin too long cause once the word gets out bout the road... jobs might get taken up purty fast," the boy said.

Ma and Pa were married only a short time, and Ma was the last to leave home, and her father said he would miss her but it would be all right if she and her new husband were to leave and look for work in south Florida.

After a month of being alone Marion Sands made the big decision to abandon his home at Henderson Creek and he too went south to look for a job on the new road. He got there too late to work on the road but was able to get a job going in front of the road crew in the swamp as a gator hunter to clear the way for the workers. This was a job that was still available because everybody thought the job was too dangerous. Mr. Sands was very good at his job and seemed to be able to keep the gators clear of where the road gang was so they didn't have to worry about getting attacked by the local vermin. He also supplied fresh meat and fish for the workers. Sands was ahead of the construction and my Ma and Pa worked at

the finished part of the road so their paths did not cross.

Later on after the road was finished my parents moved to Buzzard Bay and settled there to live after finding work on a small orange grove. They were able to live in a shack in the grove as part of the payment Pa received for working in the grove. The grove owner was elderly, not in good health and eventually he passed away and without any relatives to take over or ready cash to run the grove, the grove went wild. My Pa tried to keep up with the work for a while but without help and money to buy or fix the equipment he had to give up on the grove. After a while Pa started doing odd jobs around town to bring in enough money to care for us. This is when I was born.

The extremely rugged work that my father did for a living also made him look old for his age of twenty-seven. I knew him to be a very kind and gentle man that never raised his voice to my mother or me. He was a tall muscular man that shaved his sparsely, slow growing beard on his square chin at least once a week and seldom was seen without his palm frond hat that covered his shaggy dark brown hair. His rough callused hands were always busy doing something to eke out a living in order to take care of us. Pa did many odd jobs to make money whenever he could find work but times were hard and people didn't have any money to spare.

****

On average, we didn't catch many fish but we were grateful to pull in a few extra fish to be able to trade for other supplies at the water front town of Buzzard Bay, plus having fish for our supper table.

This day wasn't what you would call an exceptional good fishing day, the fish just didn't take much of a liken to the crab bait we were using. We did catch some white fish for supper and a couple small-stripped tiger sharks. The sharks were a commodity that we were able to make a little money. We would take the sharks and remove the inners and dry them out in the sun and then rub orange peels all over the hide to neutralize the smell. The oil from the orange peels also made the shark skin glossy and brought out the iridescent strips on the carcass stand out far better. After they were prepared properly we tried to sell them to the tourists for twenty-five cents each. Just something else I learned to do at that time.

"Most of them people ain't never seen little sharks b'fore," my Pa would say, with a twinkle in his eye.

A couple of days later Ma, Pa, and me went to town to see if we could do some trading for a few things that we needed. It was a gorgeous summer morning with just the right amount of gulf breeze to blow the sweet smell of the morning blooming wild flowers in our direction while we traveled the palm shadowed dirt road. Morning glories crept over the scrub palms and the rain lilies thrust their heads up though the spongy ground. Whooping Cranes honked loudly as they flew on their way to their feeding grounds. My mother and I skipped down the road hand in hand while Pa hummed a tune to himself.

Pa was carrying two wooden two foot by two foot "For Sale" signs under his arm. He painted these for the local Hardware store.

Old Leon, a man in his late sixties and the owner of the hardware store, preferred the way Pa painted his signs because Pa was exceptionally skillful at lettering and he also painted very pretty tropical birds on each side of the sign to fancy them up. The storeowner never paid Pa in cash but let him take provisions that we needed out in trade.

In his husky demanding tone Leon would say, " Hec... he always called my Pa that because his name was Hector and that was short for Hector. Hec, as good as ya are, ya should paint a real picture of Florida some day and I'll put it into my store to sell and if I should happen to sell it, I'll split the money with ya."

Mr. Leon S. Boxer a sweaty short over-weight man always wore the same sweat stained shirt and over-alls and had a stump of a unlit cigar sticking out of his mouth that he chewed more than he smoked. Leon was not married and lived alone and didn't have any hired help in the store. He had a unpleasant smell about him, like sour milk and leftover sauerkraut that lingered even after he left the room. Leon was a real cheap person always trying to find bits and pieces of items to sell in his store that he didn't have to put any of his money into.

But Pa told Leon he didn't like to paint that much, and that he really didn't have time for that kind of nonsense, even though Pa really had all the time in the world.

He explained to me, "If'n ya got talent to do sumpun and ya kin sell what ya make, try to sell it fer ya-self and keep all of the money. Why should ya share a part of the money with anybody?"

I think that I will always remember these important words of wisdom my Pa spoke to me for the rest of my life.

Chapter 4

At the far end of the one lane dirt road that went the twelve mile stretch through the Big Blue Cypress Swamp, off the Tam-Ami Trail, sat the historic water front town of Buzzard Bay Florida. The bay was an outlet to the Gulf of Mexico with mud shores and mangroves groping for the water, where numerous egrets were fighting for space in the branches. At the entrance to the picturesque town sat a four foot by six foot sign inviting the traveler to Buzzard Bay by claming “Best Mullet Fishing in the South”. During the rainy season the dirt road was almost impassible because the water on both sides of the road would meet in the middle and submerge it about every thirty feet. At these times Buzzard Bay was cut off from the outside world except by boat.

The notorious humidity was enhanced by the overwhelming smell that came from the mosquito infested black water, plagued with scum and algae. It wasn't until you got to the Gulf shore itself, about a mile away, before one would see the glistening white beaches and the fresh clean air with the salt breeze off the water.

Most of the laidback town consisted of several bleached white clapboard houses with the occasional stucco or white cinder block buildings and the faded gray shingled school at the far end of town. The main street stretching through the center of town was the only street that was paved and lined on both sides with large royal palms and a large variety of blooming hibiscus tropical flowers. All other streets were sand with a mixture of ground up shells and the occasional scrub palm along the edge of the street that gave off very little shade.

An open-air produce stand with racks filled with bright colored fresh oranges, lemons and grapefruit to entice the few tourists, sat next to the small grocery and pharmacy store. One whole side of the drug store had a giant red sign with drink Coca-Cola in large white letters across it and a pretty girl in a bathing suit drinking a bottle of Coke. This just happens to be the favorite beverage of the people of Buzzard Bay and the only soda sold at the soda fountain in the drug store.

Next in line to the run-down buildings was Boxer's Hardware Store that stretched to the end of the block, and where my father's painted signs could be seen in the windows. On the opposite side of the street was a two-story building with a red brick front and one large window on each side of the front door. This was a clothing store that also contained a kind of gift store where junky souvenirs could be found for the tourist trade. People that could afford to shop there could buy from a large selection of gaudy flowered shirts and shorts that matched, that they could show off to their friends back home.

We had a movie-house in town that had the most eye-appealing marquee at the entrance. There must have been at least five hundred light bulbs around their sign, but I only saw it illuminated once and was it ever beautiful. They don't light it up very often now because the cost is to much even with the price of a ticket going up to ten cents a ticket. On occasion we would peek in the door to see what was playing at the time and the smell of fresh popped popcorn escaping through the doors sure made me hungry for popcorn. They showed great films there although we never got to see any of them. Films like "Big Business" with Stan Laurel and Oliver Hardy, and "Animal Crackers" with the Marx Brothers. Also they showed "Fighting Legion" with Ken Maynard, a cowboy show, and another was "All Quiet on the Western Front" which I thought was about cowboys too until my Mother explained it was about the first World War like my Pa fought in.

Hovers five and ten a very narrow store was nudged in between the clothing store and the bank. This was my favorite place in town. My eyes would light up at the rows of penny candy and all the novelty toys on display every time we went in to look around. As I say, look around, because we seldom had any money to spend but it was always fun to look and dream of what it would be like to be able to buy something.

The First Bank of Florida was next in line with small windows and black bars over them and looked more like a jail than a bank. They had a run on the bank a couple of months earlier and there wasn't much money left in the bank if any. Two more small storefronts were adjacent to the bank but they were empty... victims of hard times. Dominic's Road Show signs were plastered all across the front of the abandoned store fronts advertising a small carnival that had come through about a year ago. The carnival only stopped at Buzzard Bay to get parts for one of the trucks that broke down, and not to set up their show. Josh Dominic, the son that took over when his father retired, felt there wasn't enough money in Buzzard to make it worth setting up the carnival but did find places in town to advertise his traveling show.

We also had a police house and a courthouse that occupied offices for the only two lawyers that practiced law in town and the local justice of peace. The mayor and the three town councilmen also had their meager offices in this building and there was a large .square room in the center of the courthouse that was used for the monthly town meeting and also substituted for a place to hold trials when needed.

The next block had a filling station on the corner with one gas pump and a rusty sign with the price of eleven cents for a gallon of gas. A location inside the building was for people to wait for the Greyhound bus that came through Buzzard Bay once a week, and a ticket stand with a small snack bar. An oil rack on the outside of the building was where the mechanic would work on cars when people who could afford to have somebody fix them. Most of the time people would do their own repairs if they could afford to buy the parts. Several cars and trucks were parked nearby that were for sale, some of which were repaired and the people couldn't afford to pay for the repairs.

Another couple businesses sat empty with doors boarded up and sporting the Dominic's Road Show signs half torn off from the weather. Houses balanced out the rest of the block with the occasional vegetable garden surrounded by unpainted picket fences that were nestled mixed between the houses. Setting at the very end the block was a small public park, with swings, see-saws, benches and picnic tables and was used mostly by tourist for picnics before they went on their way to the gulf beach. As you approached the proximity to the bay, most houses were built up on large cypress stilts to protect them from the occasional flooding from the torrential rains. The houses all had long porches around the dwelling so people could enjoy the breeze no matter where the wind was blowing.

One block over was the "Gulf Breeze Hotel." It was a stucco one story building painted a kind of coral pink

with white trim and took up the better part of the block. Colorful bougainvillea plants crawled up and over the sides of the building making an interesting contrasts to the pink walls. Along with a restaurant it had a saloon with a good size dance floor that they used in better times. A small gift shop loaded with the usual tourist junk was tucked into the right front corner of the building. Salt and pepper shakers, ashtrays, tooth pick holders, salt water taffy, penny banks, netting and some colorful sea shells that they bought from some fellow that collected them on the gulf shore and then painted the shells in bright gaudy colors.

There was an old saying about the town of Buzzard, that the sea gulls flew over Buzzard Bay upside-down because there isn't anything here worth crapping on.

"Hello sir," I started my sale pitch in a cheerful way, as I stopped a distinguished older Yankee traveler on the street in town looking up at him and smiling.

I carried the two small sharks out of sight in a palm frond basket that my Ma made. In my most impressive way I pushed my curly red hair down in the back and tried to look as cute as I could look.

"Have you heard about the good luck that would come to you if you could acquire a rare type of shark, and carry it with you while you traveled throughout the state?"

"Well... no young man," the gentleman said looking down at me.

"I never heard that story before, could you tell me more?"

I preceded to pull one of the colorful sharks out of the basket and commenced to explain to the cautious man, "Good luck only happens if the shark is a particular rare striped one and it can't be any longer than about 10 inches and is prepared in a certain way so that it brings out the mysterious good luck of the Gulf of Mexico."

The attentive curious well dressed man that seemed to be very interested in what I was telling him said, "Do you have any proof of what you are telling me?"

My eyes grew larger with the thought that the gentleman has me over a barrel and that I wasn't going to get a sale out of him. I kind of got the feeling that he was just playing me along too.

Without any hesitation, I jumped in with a big whopper of a story and said, "Just last week I talked to a lady on her way to Miami, and I explained to her the story about the good luck shark. While still doubting and hesitant to buy one of the good luck sharks, she finally broke down and offered fifty cents to acquire a shark."

"You still haven't convinced me that the shark will bring me good luck," winked the considerate man while he began to walk away.

I tugged at his coattail really thinking that I had to think fast to be sure not to lose the sale.

" I was coming to that part of the story," and hoping he would not get bored with me and continue to walk away.

Without a stop I went on, "Shortly after the lady bought the good luck shark she went to a restaurant to have supper. On the menu were fresh oysters, and that is what the lady ordered."

"Go on young man," the tolerant man said pulling out his pocket watch and checking the time.

"Well when the lady got her food order, you'll never guess what she found."

"What, go on, go on."

"Well when she opened the first oyster she found a beautiful metallic silver pearl about the size of a large pea." His eyes opened a little wider and now I could see I really had him interested, and I think I had him hooked.

I held the shark to where he could see it better and continued, "And she not only got one pearl, she found three more very high grade pearls before she was finished."

Now I was finished with my story and I could tell by the way the old man looked that he didn't totally believe me. He just stood there for a second like he was thinking. I don't know where I went wrong, if the story was too long or it just wasn't believable enough because our oysters in Florida don't have pearls. But maybe, just maybe I still had a chance.

"Now because I like you so much because you remind me of my Grandpa, I am willing to let one of my good luck sharks go for only twenty-five cents."

I thought to my self that the twenty-five cent price is all I was going to ask in the first place, but I thought the deal sounded better this way.

"Well...."

The man looked at me for another minute... put away his watch and said, "I don't care for oysters but maybe the good luck shark will bring me luck in some other way. So, I will purchase two sharks, if I may and I will pay you the whole fifty cents each for them."

I was so happy and I couldn't wait to tell Ma and Pa about my good fortune, despite the fact that I sure had to work hard for that sale.

All of the town folk thought it was funny how we took advantage of the tourist but it was some way to make a little money in these hard times.

It was reported that the kindly old Yankee that bought the two sharks from me, as he was leaving his hotel room, received a telegram from his brother telling him to come home as soon as possibly. It seems that he had a farm in Pennsylvania that they were testing to see if the land had any oil on it, and guess what? It did... and that was going to make him a very rich man. Good luck sharks... well what do you think?

Pa suggested that my mother take the dollar that I made selling the sharks and buy some needed groceries. A dollar in those days went a lot further than it does today and we were able to get two pounds of fresh peas at four cents a pound and two pounds of spinach at a nickel a pound. Also three cans of pork and beans at five cents a can along with ten pounds of red skin potatoes for eighteen cents and a nice big slab of fat-back for forty-three cents. Ma even had enough left over to buy me a small bag of my favorite striped hard candy.

That night for supper, Ma baked pan biscuits, fish, red skin potatoes and fresh peas. I can't help but laugh whenever we had peas because my Pa would always say, " I eats my peas with honey, I did so all my life, it makes the peas taste funny, but it keeps them on my knife."

Before I crawled into bed my Ma rubbed orange peels on me just like we did with the sharks, but this was to keep the mosquitoes from buzzing at me, which she did almost every night. It didn't take long before I fell asleep to dream about the events of the day.

****

Pa was busy in painting a new sign for the hardware store. A quite large three-foot by six foot sign with the name of the store in large red letters and taking up the entire space of the sign. Leon was going to replace the old weathered sign over the front door with a new impressive more legible one. Mr. Boxer gave Pa the wood and paints that Pa needed to paint the signs and Pa always had paint left over which he let me play with. I would watch my father and try to copy how he painted the various birds and sometimes I would try to paint trees and flowers to.

On this day, instead of playing with the paints, I wanted to go to the woods and hunt for baby snakes or maybe baby birds so I could have something to sell the next time we went to town. Ma was going with me to pick oranges from another run-down grove at the other side of the woods that the owner let go wild because he was to old to take care of the trees. The citrus trees did not produce many oranges of value to make it worth while to pay for the care of them. What citrus we found to pick were small but still very sweet and juicy. If Ma could find some really nice ones of good size she would polish them up and take them to town to sell or trade. We also picked wild berries when they were in season and Ma would bake the most delicious pie with them. I sure wished the berries were in season but there was no chance of that today.

When we got to the grove I helped Ma for a little while, by climbing into the rustic trees and dropping oranges to the ground. After we had an ample amount of oranges I started to look for baby snakes or birds. No luck today.

As I searched I stumbled onto an extremely large hole in the ground. As always I was quite curious to find out what was in the hole but didn't want to put my hand in and find out that it had a rattlesnake coiled up in it. I sat there very quiet for about ten minutes waiting to see if anything came out with my patience running low. The air around me was quiet and heavy and I could not hear or see any movement in the hole. Just as I was working up enough bravery to poke my hand in the strange hole, out came a little round box with four little legs under it and a stubby head stretching out as far as it could stretch, and blinking it's eyes from the bright light. It was a baby gopher box turtle undoubtedly just newly hatched. Eventually out came two more making a total of three. I still wasn't brave enough to put my hand in the hole so I don't know if there were any more box turtles in there or not.

"Ma look what I found in a hole in the field," I said very excitedly.

She said, "Calm down boy, what do ya have to tote home this time?"

"Three baby gopher box turtles," I said, putting them down in front of her.

"Ain't they just the cutest little things that you ever seen," I clamored and trying to keep them together.

"They would go real good with my pet armadillo and the baby red rat snake that I keep in a wire pen on the porch. Wouldn't they Ma? Wouldn't they?"

After all, you can't ever have too many pets to play with, I thought.

"Can I keep um? Hu, please, can I hu, can I please?" I continued.

Ma looked down at me in a way... you know the way a mother sometimes looks at you when she thinks... oh no not another critter around the house. But she knew how I liked pets so she said, "Well how about just one little critter and maybe ya kin sell the other two."

I thought to myself that my Ma was the best and she was an old softy. I was happy to be able to keep at least one of the little fellers and besides I still was able to keep the other two until we went to town again.

When we got home, Pa was putting the second coat of paint on the letters of the sign. He still had to finish with what ever birds he was going to paint on the sign but he wanted to wait until the paint dried on the letters first.

"Pa look at the cute little box turtles I found," I shouted with excitement.

"Oh boy, more critters," he said laying the sign down on the porch.

As I handed him one of the box turtles the other two scampered onto the sign and made little foot tracks across the corner of the "B" in Boxer's Hardware Emporium.

Pa said, "Oh no now I have to paint that letter over again."

I jumped up, grabbed the other two box turtles and put them in a bucket near by.

"I'm sorry Pa, I didn't think them little rascals could travel that fast. If you want me to paint the letter over, I will?"

"Son it ain't yur fault, it just shows us that turtles is faster than us."

"Do you want me to paint the letter over? Because I surely will."

"No son, I got a better idear. Let's put daisy's at the bottom of the sign and we will run a couple of them flowers up to cover up the foot prints. How would that be?"

"Pa you are so smart...I don't think that there is anything you can't do when you put your mind to it."

Chapter 5

"When we were in town, Mr. Bert Star stopped me at the hardware store and had a discussion about Timmy," said Pa while he worked on the tropical birds that he was painting on the big sign for the hardware store.

My mother looked at Pa in confusion and asked, "What did he want?"

Bert Star a six-foot tall gaunt bean pole of a man in his mid forties with a extraordinarily undersized head and lack of hair, was in charge of the only school in town. He was clean shaven except for a very narrow mustache on his upper lip and the all black set of clothes that he wore made him look more like an undertaker than a school official. Star officially was a teacher but he also took care of the clerical work at the school and made sure everything worked properly.

The one room gray cypress shingled building held classes for all the children of all ages in the area. The room was divided into three groups, one group for first through fourth grades. Another group was for fifth to the eighth grades, and the last was the smallest group, the ninth through the twelfth grades. The last group was the smallest group because not to many kids stayed in school after the eighth grade. Those children either got jobs or stayed at home to help with all the chores on the ranch. They used some of the older kids to teach and take care of the very young children.

Beside Mr. Star there was one full time teacher, Miss. Penelope Jones, and two substitute teachers that were used if they had need for them, but rarely ever needed. Miss. Penelope was of small structure a bit over weight fair skin and reddish-brown hair that she wore in a tight bun at the back of her head. She had a sweet mother like quality that helped with her teaching, especially with the younger children. The pleasant teacher traditionally wore a plain dark blue, floor length cotton dress with a bright colorful flower print apron tied around her waist. A slight touch of whimsy. She was not married but rumors were that Mr. Star was seeing her in a romantic way outside of school after hours.

Pa went on to say, "Ya know Timmy just turned seven and Mr. Star picked up on that and was wandering if'n he was gonna see him at the start of school this year. He must have found out Timmy's age by birth records in the court house."

Ma stopped what she was doing and looked intently at Pa and said, "Timmy's too small and I don't thin he's ready for this big step." And before Pa could say anything she continued, "do you really thin he has to begin this year?"

"I'm troubled so," he replied.

"Bert was quite steadfast in insisting that Timmy was going to enroll in the first grade next month."

He stopped painting on the sign that was almost finished and said, "Sides it might do him good, he can't keep playin all day long. Maybe he will like school and eventually maybe he kin learn some kind of a trade and not grow up to be as backward as his old man."

"Pa don't say that, yore not backward," she said, putting her hand on his shoulder.

"I thin ya are as smart or even smarter than most men

are, even if ya didn't git no schooling," as she tried to comfort him.

"Ya kin do things that a lot of men can't do and ya have taken very good care of us even as bad as times are," she went on.

"But maybe yore right about Timmy startin to school, it will do him good to meet other kids of his own age to play wit. It's not good for him to play alone so much, do ya realize he doesn't have any friends except his critters?" she added.

Scratching his head he said, "Yea, I guess ya are right, I will have to sit down wit Timmy tonight and break the news to him about school," he said.

"How do ya thin he'll take it, Ma?"

"Oh I'm sure he will thin it's some kind of punishment but in time he will be alright, and once he meets some other kids he will probably really like it," she said as she went back to what she was doing.

Later on that night after supper my Pa had me sit by him in his spacious somewhat soiled, rust colored overstuffed chair. I thought that I must have done something wrong because he only did this when there was something important that he wanted to talk to me about. Like the time when I put salt in the biscuit mix by mistake instead of sugar when I was helping Ma fix supper last week. Boy did those biscuits make you pucker up, but Pa never said a word, he just drank more water than normal.

"Pa are you mad that I brought home those box turtles?" I asked.

"Or maybe because I messed up the biscuits the other night?"

Pa looked at me knowing that I thought that I did something wrong and said, "No, no boy, it's not that at all, ya didn't do nothin wrong," he said trying to quench my fears, patting me on the leg.

"How would ya like to go to school?" he said.

"You mean the next time we go to town, for a visit at the school house?" I said, and I just could not understand what he meant as far as... go to school.

"No, I mean that ya would have to go to school every day," Pa replied.

"Every day? What ever would I do there every day? I clamored, with more questions in the back of my mind.

"Well, son ya will start to learn how to read for one thin, and maybe write yur name and do some numbers," Pa said trying to calm me down.

"But I already know how to write my name and I can do my numbers up to ten, what else do I need?" I said.

"I also know how to fish and take care of my critters and hunt for other critters and, and..."

I did not think that I was going to like what Pa was telling me. "How would I get there every day?" I went on.

Pa still patting me on my leg trying to assure me that it would be a good thing and said, " But ya will learn more than ya know now and ya will be able to meet other kids of yur age to play wit," he went on.

"But I don't want to meet other kids, I got all my pets," I said.

Pa still trying to explain what school was all about said, "Ya will learn about the world and be able to explore new places. I think that they will also teach ya how to draw and make pretty pictures. Won't ya like that, ya know ya like to paint pictures don't ya?"

"But Pa, I know about the woods and all the backwater, and you showed me how to draw and paint pretty pictures," I said, still reluctant to give in to this idea of going to school.

I did not want to go to school; I did not want to be

away from mother and father. I thought that I was as smart as I would ever be and I didn't need to go to school to learn any more. I was happy to play with my pets and that I didn't need to meet new kids to make any friends. I knew that they would laugh and make fun of me because I was poor. I had problems with older kids before when they picked on me and teased me when we were in town.

"I know that ya must have fears about all the new changes that will take place, but there is a teacher thar that will take care of ya ." Pa said looking directly at me.

"Miss. Penelope is a very nice person and I know ya will like her very much," he went on to say.

"Besides I'm afraid ya will have to go anyway because it's the law and I can't keep ya home even if I wanted to. The county has a truck that comes out here to pick up children that live too far from town and bring ya back home after school is out. Ya will like that, won't ya?"

I did think that getting to ride in a truck every day would be fun, but I still wasn't clear in my mind about the whole school thing.

"Will you and Ma take me to school for the first day?" I said by giving into the idea.

Pa said, " Yes if there is room in the truck for us we will come wit ya and then we kin git ya settled in at school and then come back with ya after school is out."

"Pa?" I said.

Pa looked at me and said, "What son?"

"What is a law?"

The rest of the week went on as usual. Not much was said about going to school and I even thought that Pa forgot all about it. We went fishing but just caught what we needed for our needs. Before Pa was finished with the sign he was working on, he showed me how to use your finger as an extension of the paint brush to get the feel of what you were going to paint. He even let me paint a small bird in the upper left corner of the sign. I thought it looked first-class and Pa even said that my bird was as good as what he did. Boy that statement pleased me very much. This was very important to me because whenever we went to town, I could tell people that the bird at the top left spot on the sign was painted by, yours truly, me. This also was the first time that what I painted as art would be seen by the public. Pa finished the big sign and it was a real beautiful work of art, worthy of any hardware store.

And now today I was being honored by the governor of the state of Florida for my painting. What a prestigious mark of distinction this was for me. A poor boy from a backward coastal little town in south Florida. I thought how far I have come from those days and how proud my Mother and Father would be of this honor. Oh how I wish they could be with me today. I also was thinking how hard I fought not to go to school and of the first day that I was taken to that old rustic schoolhouse.

Chapter 6

The structure looked like a haunting dark gray building covered with split cypress shingles, and a considerable amount of Spanish moss scattered across the roof from the large oak trees.

Collier county rented out the school house on Sunday to a splinter group of the United Church of the Almighty to help pay for school books and supplies for the school.

A hefty brass bell that glistened in the sun and was fastened to a large post just outside the front door. There was a older boy dressed in a checkered red and white shirt and faded blue jeans, probably around fifteen years old, tugging at a rope that made the bell sing out that it was time for the children to assemble into the one room school house. I thought to myself, how could this be happening to me?

My mother, holding my hand, passed through the double doors and passed by the boy that was clanking the bell. I wanted to put my hands over my ears to block out the sound of the bell but I was reluctant to let go of my mother.

Pa said that he would stay outside and wait for Ma on a bench under the huge southern oak tree. I could see that he was as uneasy as I was. I discovered later on in life that Pa never went to school and he wasn't to fond of schools.

The room was not brightly lit because the only light came from what came through the windows. A shoddy black chalkboard with letters on it stood in the front of the room along with a potbelly stove that would be used in case it got cold and that never happened. A small wooden table stood on each side of the teachers desk loaded down with books, pencils, paints and other supplies. There was a chair that faced the corner in the front of the room, and I didn't find out until later why it was there. Although I personally never had to sit in the chair.

We walked to the front of the room where I got my first look at Miss. Penelope Jones who was greeting another parent near her well used dark brown desk. The teacher took the boy by the hand and showed him the desk where he would be sitting and then she came back to us. My hands were as cold as ice although it was 85 degrees outside and I was terrified. The children were making so much noise that I hardly heard what my mother was saying to the teacher.

"I am Grace Dalton and this is my one and only little man, my son Timothy Dalton," She said as she let go of my hand and gently shook Miss. Jones's soft pale white hand.

I felt I was a cast aside when Ma let go of my hand so I stepped closer to her side and involuntarily latched onto her long flannel dress to give me more comfort. I held back a tear with everything in me, and just the expectation that my mother was not going to be with me for the rest of the day terrified me to no end. I thought that I was grown up but this experience drove me to doubt everything I thought. Maybe the age of seven wasn't really as mature as I was lead to believe and that I had a great deal more to learn about life. I was very close to running out of the building but I knew that Pa would not be too happy with me if I did, and I thought that I better stay no matter how afraid I was and find out just what was in store for me.

"Hello Timothy, or would you rather be called Timmy?" said Miss. Penelope Jones reaching out to me with that butter soft pale white hand.

"You do look like a nice big grown up young man," she said.

Miss Jones said it too, "Big grown up man."

Is this a phrase that all adults say to kids or does she, like my parents, actually think that I am truly a grown up person?

"Hello Miss. Jones," I said in an extremely shaky voice still holding onto Ma's dress and not about to let go.

"Will you please follow me and I will show you to your desk," she said.

She still held onto my hand as we walked to the desk and I was still holding onto my Ma almost dragging her along with us. Some of the older children chuckled as the parade went by them and I felt even more terrified. Once we got to the desk everybody let go of each other and I sat down in a huge worn-out dark chocolate oak desk. My feet did not touch the floor and I had to push myself all the way forward just to be able to reach the top of the desk.

Ma stayed with me for a few minuets more until the teacher got all of the classes to calm down and had all of us to introduce our self to the rest of the classes.

“This is going to be a short day today and ya will only be here until noon,” Ma said, trying to assure me that it wasn’t going to be as bad as I thought it was.

“Pa and me will be back at noon and then the truck will take us back home,” she went on to say.

“I love you Mama,” I said almost thinking that I wasn’t ever going to see her again.

“I love ya too son,” she said as she bent down to kiss me on the top of my head. “It really is goin to be all right, Timmy,” she said calming my fears.

I can not tell you how small and distressed I was at that time. For the first time in my life I did not have either one of my parents within eyeshot of me and it almost made me sick. How I managed to stay in my seat until the bell rang to end the school for the day, I surely don’t know. I shot out of my seat and out of the building before anyone else and I ran to my mother and clung to her as if there was no tomorrow. My first day of school was over.

The truck took us home and I was as quiet as a church mouse. Ma and Pa didn't say anything either. I thought for now they didn't want to bring up the frightening experience that I went through today and they wanted me to just forget about it. I know today that this was the worst thing that I ever experienced in my life at the age of seven but I had no idea of what the future held for me.

Monday morning jumped up at me like a rattlesnake striking at a possum. It stormed last night, a real wind choker, but it was a very beautiful and calm day now. I just finished a plate of grits and gravy and Ma also fixed some fatback, something special for the occasion I figured. This was the first full day of school and I was going to be all by myself the whole day.

"Put on your best overalls and the clean shirt that I laid out for ya," Ma said.

"And ya will have to wear yore shoes agin today;" she said urging me on.

"Oh Ma," I said.

"Don't oh Ma me, ya know ya have to wear shoes to school. They won't let ya in the school if ya don't have shoes on," she explained.

"And don't even thin about taking yore shoes off when ya git to school."

I rebelliously finished getting dressed and then went out to check on my pets.

I had to be up on the road by 7a.m. this morning to be sure to get a ride on the truck that would take me to town.

Ned the driver was going to come by at 7:15 a.m. and beep the horn once and if I wasn't there he wouldn't wait, he would just go on to the next stop without me.

I was at the spot where I would be picked up by 7:00 a.m. with Ma by my side reassuring me while we waited for the truck that everything was going to be okay.

Ma said, "It sure is a beautiful day, a really good day to start school. Today ya will recollet and cherish fer the rest of yore life."

"But Ma couldn't it be next year or next month or even next week after I get my courage up?" I pleaded.

"I am sure there will be more beautiful days later on," still pleading but loosing the battle.

"Nope, it has to be today, right now, right on this cheer beautiful day," She insisted, knowing that I didn't have anything to say about the matter, and she didn't have a say in it either as far as that goes.

The sun was sending silver splinters dancing through the branches of the trees when the wind blew. Mocking birds jumping from limb to limb made their tropical cries to welcome in the new day. Squirrels played hide and seek in the brush around the cabbage palms. And yes, my mother was right, it was a captivating day. A sunrise that an artist would beg for and just one more day that made my life so wonderful. The truck arrived exactly at 7:15 a.m. Ma kissed me on the head and patted me on my back and I started to step on the truck.

"Ma?" I said as I gave her my best sorrowful look one last time.

"Ya will be just fine," she said, taking in my big mournful eyes and trying to force back a tear in her own.

"It will be over before ya know it and I will have some fresh baked cookies waitin fer ya when ya git home," she said as she stepped back away from the truck.

Ned took one look at me, never said a word just snorted and jerked the vehicle forward which threw me to a seat. A large puff of bluish-gray smoke belched out of the back of the truck as we bounced down the road.

The driver smoking a hand rolled cigarette was a very disordered unkempt man in his mid fifties, with skin like old tanned wrinkled raw hide. He was unshaven and his bib-overalls had the workings and foul stench of a freshly skinned deer covering the front of him. He wore boots that went up to his knees that were full of mud. The brimless hat that he wore barely covered his long unruly, greasy gray hair.

The school bus really wasn't a truck, actually it was a cross between a large noisy car and a chopped up rusty green truck. It had three rows of seats made out of strips of hard wood and had all of the windows taken out so that it wouldn't get too hot. There wasn't any protection against the rain in foul weather.

Three children were on the truck, twin girls about the age of twelve and a older boy about fifteen years old, when I got on the noisy vehicle. The boy was the one that laughed at me Friday in school when I went to my seat.

Ned had to be a very good driver because of the way he was able to run in and out of every road furrow that there was and still not lose control of the vehicle.

We only stopped to pick up four other kids, all girls much older than me, before we got to school. It took about thirty-five minutes to arrive at the school and it would have taken about an hour and fifteen minutes by walking.

I would find out later that it was the older girls job at the school to sweep the floors daily and help keep the room clean. Older girls also had to help with smaller children too. It was the job of the older boys to move the desks out of the way on Friday night so that the room would be ready for the church assembly on Sunday. Then they had to be at school a few minutes early on Monday to put everything back to normal for the start of school. It was also their duty to fix anything small that had to be taken care of that didn't call for a carpenter to fix. This system seemed to work so that the county wouldn't have to pay for a full time custodian.

I went to my assigned seat and didn't say anything to anybody, not even Miss. Jones. By the end of the day I realized that school really wasn't all that bad but I still wasn't convinced that I liked it very much. I thought that I could put up with gaining an education to please my mother and father if I had to.

Chapter 7

Summer dragged into winter like the print in the naked white sand left by a lazy old slim green gator sliding into the swamp... long... and very slow moving.

Pa worked on an oil lamp that he was repairing for a lady that lived down the road from us. The sixty-six year old woman discovered that my father did odd jobs from the owner of the hardware store and she was having all her hurricane lamps changed over to electricity. She was in the process of having electricity run into her house after she came into some money from an inheritance and now she was considered the richest lady in south Florida. Pa was going to get paid in cash so he couldn't pass up the job and was happy for the work. The lady was also considering having Pa paint her whole house inside and out. This would be a wonderful thing because he would be finished with the job just before Christmas and when he got paid he would have money for the holiday. My parents did the best they could but Christmas was just a name in the month of December. We were very poor and presents of any kind at any time, were a rarity but this was all going to change this year.

Ma was content to fish at water edge to put what she could on the supper table. The fish in the backwater was mostly junk fish like gar and catfish but with enough seasonings Ma managed to make them tasty.

Miss Jones dished out lessons like so many doses of castor oil. I was settling into school but I could hardly wait to get home each day to my pets and the place that I was most comfortable.

"Timmy what did ya learn in school today?" Pa would always say as soon as I got home.

"Well let me see, I learned my numbers up to twenty and some more of A B C's."

"But you want to hear the best thing that happened to me today?" I asked with excitement today.

"Of course I do."

"We were having drawing time and I drew an egret

and when Miss. Penelope saw it, she said it was the best she ever saw. Then you know what she did?"

"Well what did she do son?" Pa said kind of impatiently.

I brought out the drawing of the bird with the real pretty blue star stuck to it at the top and showed it to Pa.

"She showed it to the whole school and then she had me explain how to draw the bird to everybody and then everybody had to try and draw it," I said just bursting with pride.

"Ma come over cheer and look at Timmy's purdy picture," Pa said.

My mother stopped what she was doing and said, "Timmy, that bird is better than what Pa kin do, and I am so proud of ya and how well ya are doin in school. Don't ya thin so Pa?" she said.

Father looked at my Mother and saw a look on her face that said, tell the boy how proud you are of him. Then he put down what he was working on and smiled at me.

"I am very proud of ya Timmy and now would ya show me how ya drew the egret so I do it the right way the next time and then will ya count to twenty for me," he said.

"And you know what else?" I said in a sheepish shy way.

Ma seemed to be the most interested in that question and replied back, "What else is on yur mind?"

"I met a new friend today on the play ground," I said.

My mother was so excited that I was making new friends and asked, "Oh...what is the little boys name?"

I looked at her and replied, "It's not a boy, it's a girl and her name is Rose Bud Benton."

"A girl! Well ain't that nice. Rose Bud Benton...aha! My big boy is becoming a man in a hurry, ain't he Pa?"

Pa turned to go back to what he was doing and just shrugged his shoulders.

I wondered what she meant by that, after all Rose Bud was just a girl not some wild animal that I would have to tame.

"Is she purty?" My mother asked with a question that didn't make any sense to me.

"She is a girl and there ain't nothing pretty about that," I said.

"She was watching me draw birds and flowers when we had play time and she said that she liked watching what I was doing and stayed with me the whole period. She also asked me if I wanted to share some of her apple that she brought for lunch."

"Did ya share?"

"Sure I did, I wasn't going to turn down an apple, even if I had to share it with a girl."

But at last, after only a few days, I lost my first girl friend to Samuel Brown. Sammy had a likable red pony that he rode to school and that made him a very popular person with all of the kids, especially with Rose Bud Benton. Samuel Brown would give pony rides during play time and that was all it took to lose my friend. Oh well, easy come, easy go. I thought that the only thing I could do was draw a picture of the pony but that still couldn't get Rose Bud Benton back. Rose Bud Benton was just another kid with a girls name and I didn't put anything into that.

Our family bonds were so powerful, at that time, it was almost spiritual. I thought that my parents would always be there for me and protect me.

Finally the last day of school before the Christmas holiday was here and when I got off the truck and walked toward the house I could feel something different in the air. I could hear my mother humming a Christian tune, something I haven't heard her do in a long time. I entered the house and I found my mother putting brightly colored paper stars, that she cut out of construction paper, all over the house. Pa was busy setting up a small scrub pine in the center of the main room.

"Pa what is all this," I said after greeting my folks. I knew about Christmas from the kids in school but we never celebrated it before at home.

"Its Christmas, son, and we are goin to have a good holiday meal and maybe some surprises too," Pa said in a very happy tone.

"Isn't it wonderful Timmy?" Ma said as she started to string red and green ribbon on the small tree?

"Want to help?" Pa asked.

"I sure do, what can I do?" I clamored all excited.

"Ya kin help yore ma put on the ribbon and some of those little stars she cut out and I'll git a fire started to roast this handsome chicken that we got in town today," Pa said.

When we ran out of stars Ma said, "Timmy ya kin cut some more stars out and I will try to hang some oranges on the tree and then I am goin to start bakin a sweet tater pie."

The tree turned out to be a real work of art. I cut more stars out and put them on the tree and then I drew some birds and cut them out and put them on the tree. My parents were like they were in another world. I had never seen them this way before and I wanted this time to last forever. Mother wove a really attractive hat for my Father and Pa carved a pair of candle holders that looked like they had birds on them for my Ma. We ate one of the best meals that I could ever remember and was setting back to have a large piece of sweet potato pie when Ma brought a new pair of shoes and a set of clothes that they bought for me with some of the money that Pa made painting the ladies house. Mama also made me some real chocolate candy, something I was not accustomed to but enjoyed very much. Pa also gave me his lucky silver dollar that his Pa gave him when he was a boy about my age. A coin that he carried all through the time he was in the army. My father almost rubbed the feathers off the bird on the back of the dollar but it still was impressive. His Pa told him as he told me that if I would keep this silver dollar and not spend it, that I would never be broke.

I ate my pie and then I asked if I could have another piece of candy.

"Sure ya kin but ya have one more surprise," she said, walking over to a box in the corner.

She picked up the box and I thought for a moment that the box seemed to jerk in her hand as if something was alive in the box. She set the box on the floor by me and told me to open it. I hesitated with uncertainty.

"Go on open it up, I know ya will like it," Pa said.

I could tell it was something alive but I wasn't prepared for what jumped out. A lump of furry coal with four legs and two big yellow eyes.

My Ma told me when they were in town they saw a feller that was giving away kittens and Pa decided that I would like to have one, so he picked out a beautiful coal black boy kitten.

"What are ya goin to call yore new little friend?" Pa asked.

I looked at my Mother and Father and then thought for a minute and said, "I am going to call him Little Tom."

I was hugging my new pet and didn't want to put him down.

"Why are ya goin to call him Little Tom?" Pa said.

Ma jumped in on the conversation and said in excitement, "Oh I thin I know why! Ya want to call him Tom because he is a tomcat and little because he is so small, am I right?"

"Yes you are right, you are so smart."

And I hugged Ma with Little Tom between us.

Pa said, "Yu two are so much alike that I am sure that Timmy is yur son. Ya know God knew He could not be everywhere so He made mothers to be there fer her children."

Tears of happiness formed in my eyes as the black kitten purred in my lap and licked the chicken oil off from my fingers. My love shines for this new playmate like the silver dollar that my father gave me.

Sometime in February Pa got several different types of seeds in trade for some work he did at the hardware store. He tilled the sandy soil beside the house out in the full sun with hopes of starting a garden. He wasn't patient enough to maintain the meager garden and soon gave up the duties to Ma and me. The warm winter sun brought the seeds to sprout in just a few days along with a large variety of weeds that keep me busy after school trying to pull out what I thought were weeds.

Little Tom was learning his name and ran to me as soon as I got off the truck. By the time the vegetable sprouts were big enough to tell what they were we learned that we were not meant to be farmers. What the squirrels didn't eat the swamp rats did and Little Tom spent most of the day while I was in school chasing them with not much luck because of his size.

Then we had the infestation of the truly unusual bugs with the most destructive jaws and that was pretty much the end of the garden. Ma did manage to save one tomato plant by putting a wire screen over the plant and we actually got five tomatoes in all that turned out to be very good. What ever you do with your parents when you are young effects everything you do the rest of your life.

****

In the top of the tallest oak tree in the forest, just on the edge of the black swamp lived one of the largest bald eagles in undomesticated Florida. His well-built nest consisted of his partner and two chicks that were hatched out two weeks earlier. So far the parents fed the young a variety of fish caught in the backwater, swamp rats, rabbits and just what ever they could swoop down and carry back to the nest. Today was one those days the majestic male was on the search for some more baby food.

Little Tom was on the prowl still trying to keep the squirrels and swamp rats clear of the garden. Once he was brave enough to jump at a white tailed long-eared rabbit that was hunkered-down under a palmetto at the edge of the garden. I was at school and my mother and father were out on the dingy fishing.

The huge eagle soared hundreds of feet over the house and with his keen sense of sight he could scan everything below on the ground. Something black and shinny zipped across the opening in front of the house below that looked interesting. With the ease of a wooden glider falling at the rate of forty miles an hour, he dove at Little Tom. The kitten jumped in a split second just as the giant bird with the five foot wing span grabbed at the cat and came up with nothing but air. The bird flapped his giant wings that took him soaring back to his station in the sky to prepare for the next charge at the cat.

Within an instant the attack was on again. The black cat sensed that another assault was coming and in confusion scampered to the house just before the eagle hit the sand. Little Tom let out a shrieking squeal acting like an all grown lion but still shaking all over. Back to the sky went the eagle to plan his next approach. The black cat not able to get into the house raced toward a group of cabbage palms on the edge of the clearing.

Once more the giant predator honed in on Little Tom just as a noisy green truck stopped on the road. Timmy jumped off the truck and saw the bird of prey charging down on Little Tom. Timmy ran to the clearing and took

off one of his new shoes and threw it at the bird barely missing him. The sleek black cat ran to Timmy with his heart beating uncontrollably. Little Tom was safe and the sky was empty of the giant bird once more and only Timmy and Little Tom knew what happened.

Chapter 8

Spring sprang with the sweet fragrance of orange blossoms blooming in the abandoned run down grove. When I was out of school my mother and I spent hours in the grove when it was in bloom. I would hunt for small snakes and baby birds or climb trees with Little Tom right with me everywhere I went. My mother would take in the beauty of the weather and the delicate scent of the grove and sit underneath a tree and read a book.

****

Grace had four brothers and five sisters that along with her parents lived in small poor country town in central Florida on about one acre of unforgiving, sand-covered scrub land.

The small town of Henderson Creek was established for Civil War veterans from both Union and Confederate soldiers. The founding fathers felt there was a need to bring these wayward soldiers together in a place that they could start a new life and put the terrible war behind them, a place that everyone could live in peace and try to build there lives over again. In order to entice them to settle here they were offered, by an unscrupulous real-estate company, a one acre plot free if they would buy a one acre plot and settle there. This was one way the greedy realtor was able to unload his worthless scrub land and still make it look like a good deal to the unsuspecting customer. Several veterans purchased land this way and then sold off the free lot at a much cheaper price just to help cover part of what they paid on their lot. These cheap lots were known as throw-offs. Mr. Marion Sands and his wife Jules lived on one of these throw-off lots and this is where they tried to raise their ten children.

Marion had few skills and barely scraped out enough food from this land to feed all the children. He tried planting some tobacco but the sandy soil was not adequate for that crop, so what he settled on was sweet potatoes and vegetables. The children were trained to do many things to make themselves knowledgeable and self -sufficient. The boys learned to help with the crops, fish, hunt game and how to skin and tan the hides. My Ma, along with all the other girls, were taught to sew, and also weave scrapes of cloth together to make rugs that they traded for other items at the general store. Her Pa also showed her the art of weaving palm fronds into sun hats. This lost art was important because most people wore some sort of sun hats and my Ma made the best hats and they were always in demand.

The uncharacteristic town was sparsely populated and had very few decent stores and practically no professional citizens. One very important person would have been a doctor, if they had one. The only general-store in town had a limited supply of drugs and the majority of people relied on old-fashion natural remedies to treat most illness anyway.

One hot summer, the girls had accumulated an over abundance of hats and hand made rag-rugs. After trading what they could in town they still had too many left over, so Mr. Sands told Holly, the oldest girl, and my Ma to take them to Cranes Roost to see if they could sell what they had left. Cranes Roost was about twenty five miles away and my Ma was very excited to be traveling to a larger town. So bright and early just before the sun rose the next day, with rugs strapped to Holly's back and Grace carrying the hats, they set off to the big town. They arrived at Mr. and Mrs. Hager's house very late that night. The Hager's received a letter from their dear old friend Mr. Sands and was asked if they would take care of his girls while they were in Cranes Roost. Early the next morning Mr. Hager took the girls to the large trading store and introduced them to the owner. He was so impressed with the quality of their goods that he bought all they had right there on the spot.

"What are you girls going to do with all this money," said the store owner counting out several silver dollars.

Holly started to speak and was interrupted by Mr. Hager, "I think that most of the money will go to their Pa who's having a hard time making ends meet right now."

But before they go home I'm going to take them to the Traveling Carnival Show that wintered here in Florida and was setting up just outside of town.

The girls were very happy and excited with their sales and couldn't wait to get home to tell their Pa.

The two girls barely slept a wink that night thinking about the Carnival that they were going to the next day. They knew that their Pa wouldn't be mad if they stayed a couple of days longer because of the great sales that they had. The next day, after a big breakfast, Mr. and Mrs. Hager loaded up a picnic lunch and everybody went to the Carnival. After a long fun filled exhausting day at the fair they went home and the two girls fell asleep early. They stayed one more night with the Hager's and then returned home late the next morning.

The same day the girls left to go to Cranes Roost, the Newman boy down the road from the Sands, got sick and died very suddenly. Without any knowledge of the disease that had infected him, the disease started spreading very fast. The fever crept from house to house grabbing whoever it pleased. Young... old... men... women... even children, until it seemed like the whole town was infected by the strange illness.

The oldest boy of the Sands family, a boy of thirteen, was the first to become sick when the outbreak of Yellow fever raced through the town. Today a disease like that could be stopped in its tracks, but it wasn't like that then... no doctors... no drugs. Some house-holds were lucky and some weren't. It just happened that the Sands family wasn't one of the lucky ones.

At least one or more person in every house-hold were taken down with the fever and died. My Ma's family was one of the hardest to be infected by the fever. My Mother has always been reluctant to talk about the disease that took her mother, three brothers and two sisters to the Lord.

Holly and Grace were very happy and couldn't wait to show their Pa how much money they collected for the goods that they sold. They sold everything in one place and the owner of the department store said he would take more, especially the hats, whenever they had more to sell. Also the price they received was much higher then they expected.

"What is that wagon a'blocking the road"? Holly said, when the girls arrived at the edge of town.

Two large men with long rifles in their hands and a very nasty look on their faces jumped out from the wagon and pointing the rifles at them said, "Who are ya girls and what business do ya have cheer?"

The girls clutched each other in fear thinking they were going to be robbed of their new found wealth and said, "We live cheer. Our Pa is Marion Sands and we live just on the other side of town, just down from the Newman's."

"What ya girls doin out cheer at this time of day?" said the meanest looking one of the two men still pointing his intimidating rifle at them.

"How did ya girls get past the guards anyway?" the other one said.

"Mister can I ask ya a question?" Holly said.

"Ya didn't answer my question and I wants to know what ya are doin cheer?" said the mean looking man.

"We went to Cranes Roost to sell some hats and hand made rugs and we are just now gittin back."

Ma spoke up and said, "And we want to go home. Why caint we go home?"

"Thars ben an outbreak of yellow fever in town and nobody is coming in and nobody is going out, so you best just turn round and head back to where ya-all come from."

"But we live here and we have to go home to see if everybody is okay," Holly said in tears.

The two girls started to walk around the wagon and the man with a scowl on his face grabbed Holly by the arm and pulled her back.

"Yur not goin anywhere girlie," he said.

"I told ya to just go back to the town ya just came from caus ya ain't comin through cheer," the other man said as he grabbed my Ma.

By now the two girls were in tears and didn't know what to do. They were very worried about their family and they were also frightened for their well being.

"But we can't go back, we have to go home," my Ma cried.

"Don't ya understand?"

Just as the men were pushing the girls back another man came walking up behind the wagon and said, "Take your hands off them girls, what's the matter with you men?"

"They's trying to get through the blockade," as the men let go of the girls.

"They say they live down the road on the other side of town but we didn't believe them."

"They do live here. This cheer is Mr. Sands youn-guns," the man said as he walked up to the girls and took off his hat to them.

"Are you gals okay? They didn't hurt ya did they?"

"No, we are fine but we have to get home and see if our folks are okay."

"I think it will be acceptable, we haven't had anymore deaths recently. I'll take them home now," said the nice man taking the girls by their hand.

The man walked them right up to the house to make sure that the girls made it home without any trouble. The only boy left alive came to the door and said he was so happy that the girls were home . They all went into the house and the girls heard all the bad news.

Her Pa was very depressed after that for a long time and as soon as her brother and sisters were able to move away, they did. When my Mother met my Pa she was the last to leave. Her father had never fully recovered from the loss of so many of his children nor especially his wife. He felt that there wasn't anything to keep him at Henderson Creek, with all the bad memories and all, so he finally moved away too. Over time, Ma lost contact with him and didn't know if he was living or dead.

****

From time to time Ma would ask me to cut some

palm fronds and she would pass the time of day by practicing the art of weaving sun hats that she learned as a little girl. By stripping scrub palm fronds into small strips she was also able to weave several varieties of folk art baskets that she would take along with the sun hats to the hardware store and trade for supplies. On occasion I would bring scraps of wood and some paints to the grove to paint small pictures. I tried to paint birds and the different kinds of palms that I saw in the grove. Pa would teach me what he knew about mixing the different paints to get the various colors. It amazed me how many colors you can obtain by mixing only a few different colors together.

Chapter 9

"Come on Honey, hurry up and finish yur breakfast it's gettin late," Ma said helping me get ready for school.

"Ma, I can't go any faster," I said.

"Oh yes ya kin, and ya better not be late for that thar truck or ya will have to use yur feet as a truck to get to school," Ma continued.

Pa came into the room and said, "When ya git home from school today I have a job fer ya to do."

"What's that Pa?"

"I have to paint a small sign for Leon and I thin I can trust ya to do it fer me. Yore Ma and me have to go out on the Gulf to try and catch a few nice tuna for the grocery store and we have to go a ways out so I don't have time to paint the sign. We might not be here when ya git home so don't worry bout us."

"What do you want me to put on the sign, Pa?" I questioned.

Pa brought the one foot square board out and the paints and said, "Leon wants to starts sellin bait to the tourist to fish wit, so he just wants the sign to read BAIT FOR SALE, in large letters. Use the red paint for the letters on the white board."

I looked at the board and said, "Can I paint some small fish on the board too?"

"Yea, that would be okay as long as ya makes the letters as big as ya kin first. Member the main reason for the sign is to tell the people what ya are sellin, not the pretties that ya put on it," Pa said trying to explain the art of painting signs.

"I'll do it just the way you would do it Pa," I said. "You can trust me, Pa. I'll put the letters on first and if it would look right with a few little fish on it I will put them on after, would that be okay?"

"Yep son, that would be fine, I know I kin trust ya to do a good job," Pa said assuring me.

"Come on Timmy," Ma said, still tryin to hurry me up.

" Thar is some corn bread and oranges if you git hungry if'n we're not back til late."

I walked up to the road where the truck was just pulling up and I had just enough time to kiss Ma good by.

As I got on the truck I heard Ma said, "Have a good day, I love ya my big boy."

"I love you to," I said and the kids all snickered.

The sky was very strange for this time of year. There were no clouds and the color of the sky was an unfamiliar yellow tone. The sun was stretching upward but not very radiant. By the time we got to the school the sky had changed to weird orange color, the color of a ripe orange and there seemed to be a lazy haze covering the sun. About one o'clock, half way through our numbers it

started to rain and within ten minutes the sky turned reddish-black and it was like the devil himself was throwing buckets of water on us. I've seen it rain hard before, even went through a small hurricane once but not anything as unusual as this. Some of the small children and a few of the older girls started to whimper with the downpour.

Miss. Jones tried to calm everybody down by saying, "Sit down in your seats; the rain will be over in just a few minutes."

The rain by now was hitting the panes of glass in the windows so hard that water was starting to come in through the cracks. Just then one of the windows closest to me blew inward missing me by inches. The window came crashing to the floor smashing into a million pieces. That certainly got my attention and the little girl next to me let out such a screeching scream that it started a chain reaction from several other children around us to scream too. The little girl was crying because she got cut on her arm by a stray piece of broken glass. The injury was not serious but the way she was crying you would have thought her arm was cut off.

Miss Jones came rushing to us with a clean towel to wrap the little girls arm with. As soon as she made the girl comfortable, and made sure nobody else was hurt she took off her apron and shouted to two of the older boys, "Bob and Jeff help me cover the window with my apron."

Just then, like we were being attacked by some unidentified furious force, the door flew open and blew all of the papers off of our desks and the girl closest to the door jumped out of her seat and ran to the back of the room. That brought on more screams from others in the room and more kids got out of their seats and started to run around the room. Lightning was striking all around the school and finally found it's mark on the great oak tree in the front of the building making such a noise that it rattled and vibrated the whole schoolhouse. Lightning continued to light up the sky and made a fluorescent hue over the school.

Big eyes of some of the smaller children peered out from under their desk where they scrambled for protection, but not me. No not me... because I was too grown up to be afraid. We could hear an enormous thud from one of the branches falling to the ground and another branch being slammed onto the top of the roof. The older boys hurried to the door to look out to see what happened.

Miss. Jones rushed to them and pulled the door closed and said, "Back to your seats children. Becky calm down. You, Carla and Brenda help me get everybody back to his or her seats."

"I am sure everything is going to be okay," she called out with a tinge of fear in her voice.

"Jeff please get those children back to their seats in the back of the room."

The building rattled unrelenting and lightning flashed violently and children in spite of all of the coaching were weeping and some would not come out from under their desks.

Rainwater was now seeping through at the spot where the branch punched a hole through the roof making more of an unpleasant situation.

I could hear loud noses as shingles were being jerked from the building and thrown into the trees.

As if a large hand reached out and pulled the school bell from it's post and slammed it against the schoolhouse, and then picked it up again and slammed it into the building over and over until it finally bounced out into the school yard and rolled to a rest by the scrub palms.

"Children please calm down," shouted the now terrified teacher that looked like she was trying to find a place that she could hide as well.

Now I was just the least bit afraid, wondering how long this storm was going to last. I had to admit to myself that I wished my Mother was here with me to hold me and protect me.

The schoolhouse continued to rattle and I thought that pressure inside was about to pull the walls apart, nail by nail.

With the wind still blowing like there was no tomorrow and still ripping shingles from the building a strange thing started to take place. The rain stopped. Miraculously within ten minutes of the rain stopping, the wind let up and the storm seemed to be over. We all jumped up to look out the windows to see what it looked like outside.

Tree limbs were thrown about everywhere and water made great gouges in the ground ending in vast puddles. The great oak tree was split in three sections with one large branch resting on the top of the school roof.

"Stay in the building until I can see if it is safe to go

outside," shouted Miss. Jones as she slowly pried open the door.

She struggled to open the door but as she did she found it to be blocked by a tree branch.

"Johnny Stokes will you climb out a window and come around to clear the doorway so I can get out?" said the teacher.

Johnny was the biggest boy in the school and he was built like a full grown man. If anybody could do it Johnny could.

"I can do it Miss. Jones," said Johnny as he pulled what was left of the apron off the window and crawled out.

"I want to help too," said Bob wanting to get out of the building as soon as possible.

Miss. Jones said, "Okay but that's it, nobody else go out. I don't want everybody climbing out the window."

By the time Johnny Stokes and Bob got the limbs moved from the doorway, three men from town came running to help.

"Is everyone okay," said one of the men while another looked inside the schoolhouse and the third helped Miss. Jones outside?

"We are all fine, just shook up and a little frightened," replied Miss. Jones.

The man helping Miss. Jones was Mister Star and he said, "I already contacted Ned to bring the school bus over here and get these children home as soon as possible."

"Was that a hurricane?" said Miss. Jones.

"No, I don't think so, just a freak wild storm," said Mr. Star. "There was very little damage down town, looks like you got the brunt of the storm here," he continued.

"Let's make sure the children are all okay," Miss. Jones said. "Sara Strum has a small cut on her arm but I think she is okay."

By the time we all got out of the building, the truck was there to take the children home and the rest of the children were told to go straight home and not to play in the water-puddles on the way home.

The wind picked up a little again with sporadic shards of rain that pelted us through the windows of the truck. The ride home was rough as the truck leaping in and out of the ruts that the water made in the road but I was glad to be going home.

Chapter 10

"Ma, Pa, did it storm here as much as it did in town?" I yelled as I ran to the house.

I noticed that there wasn't any water standing in large puddles and it didn't appear to be much if any tree or palm damage to the surrounding scrubs. Moreover there was no damage to the house and Little Tom was dry when he came running to me.

"Where is everybody?" I asked Little Tom.

"Oh that's right, the dinghy was gone and Ma and Pa were probably still out fishing," I told Little Tom picking him up into my arms.

Oh I remember now Pa asked me to paint the sign for Mr. Boxer that would have the words "BAIT FOR SELL" on it if I got home before they did. And because of the storm, I did get home early. Boy, wait until they get home, what a story I was going to tell them about the fierce storm we had while I was at school.

"Well I better get to painting the sign," I told my furry pet.

Halfway through painting the letters I decided to stop and get a bite to eat. I recalled Ma telling me there was some corn-bread in the bread box if I got hungry, so I ate a piece of that and then an orange. I also found a piece of dried fish and I gave that to Little Tom. After I ate I checked on Mr. Armadillo, the baby box turtles and my pet red rat snake and then went back to working on the sign.

I got the letters finished and they really looked great, now to paint some cute little fish around the sign. A few minuets later the sign was finished but there still was no sign of my parents.

"Maybe they are just doing so good fishing that they are using the extra time to see if they can catch more than they need," I told Little Tom as I cleaned up the paints and brushes.

I checked the seven-day clock in the house and it was half past seven and the sun was putting a low red glow in the sky. Setting on the steps of the porch I looked longingly over the water to see if I could see any indication of my parents in the dinghy. But thirty minutes later there was no sign of them.

“What do you think we should do Little Tom?” I said.

“I think I am going to have another piece cornbread and see if there is anything else to eat.”

By now it was getting pretty dark and I was very concerned that something might have happened to my parents. Little Tom and I went inside and put a match to the oil lamp and brought it back outside so my parents would have a light to come home by. The moths and night insects swarmed around the light and after a short time, I fell to sleep listening to the tune of the whip-o-wills. Day light brought on a new day with no sign of my parents. I held onto Little Tom and started to sob.

“Where are they,“ I said between tears to my pet cat.

By seven o’clock I had to decide if I was going to school or stay home and wait for my folks to come home.

I stayed home.

I was hungry but I didn’t want to take my eyes off the backwater hoping to see my parents at anytime. About noon and a lot of tears later I figured I better do something so I took Little Tom and started walking to the bay.

Arriving at the bay I could see a great deal of damage to the trees and a lot of debris washed on the shore. I walked as far as I thought I should but there was still no sign of Ma and Pa or the dinghy so I started to go back home. On the way home I stopped at the grove and filled my pockets with oranges and ate two on the way.

At home my hopes were shattered when I found nobody there and I was now beyond being scared. I was terrified... my face was hot and wet with tears and my eyes were sore, red and swollen so that I could hardly see. I felt lost and confused and I didn't know what to do or where to go. My mind was filled with dreadful thoughts.

I lit the lamp again and sat on the steps holding Little Tom, and again was caressed by night creatures until I fell asleep once more.

The next morning I avoided the school truck on the road and stayed home from school again. I didn't want to be away if Ma and Pa came home, knowing they would want me to be here waiting for them.

The sound of a car engine knocking to a stop up on the road jarred me to my senses and as I rubbed my eyes

I could see a tall stranger walking toward the house. The man was Chester Pool one of the men that came to the school to help out after the storm and was the only person that served as a policeman in the village of Buzzard Bay.

"Are you Timothy Dalton?" the man said as he approached the house.

My first thought was to run because I thought he was coming to take me to jail for skipping school for the last two days. You know because of the *law.* This was just another bad thought crammed in my already over crowded mind.

He looked at me without any facial expression, did not smile... and his tone of voice was that of strength and authority.

"My name is Chester Pool and I serve as a policeman from Buzzard," the man spoke, looking down at me with his deep dark eyes.

I got up to run to the scrub palms and tripped over the cat and went down to my knees in the soft sand.

"Wait son, reaching down to help me up. I'm not going to hurt you. I know you haven't been in school for the last couple of days, but that is not why I am here," he said brushing sand off of me with his large rough hands.

"I'm here to talk to you about your parents," he said now with a softer tone in his voice.

"My Ma and Pa?" I said, eager to hear any news about them.

"Have you seen them? Do you know where they are? Why haven't they come home?"

I fired one question after another to the policeman, not giving him enough time to answer any of the questions that I asked.

He toned his voice down and spoke to me in a kinder manner and his face broke a smile now, and he said, "No, I haven't seen them but we need to talk. Please can we sit down?"

He placed his large strong hand on mine and nudged me toward the shack. He was more pleasant now as he tried to console me and put me at ease.

"Do you want to go inside?" I asked.

"No, the steps will be fine, if that's all right with you."

Already I was beginning to calm down as we took a seat on the step of the small porch. Little Tom came to me and curled up into my lap and started to purr.

"You said you haven't seen them but do you know where they could be?" I questioned.

"No ... but Timothy there is a dingy that was found damaged in the Mangroves about two miles south of the bay. The numbers that were on the boat were registered to your father, and you say they haven't been home?"

"No."

Now with fear coming back again and more bad thoughts bouncing around in my head I said, "What does that mean?"

"I don't know at this time... maybe nothing. Maybe they saw the storm coming and came ashore on one of many of the small islands around and some how their boat got away from them," he said.

"Who has been taking care of you?"

I looked at him and in my mind I questioned why he was asking that.

"Well, I can take care of myself, sir," I said.

"I am sure you can and I bet you do a good job. I think at this time that everything is okay, your parents must have been caught on one of the small islands in the storm, and like I said their boat must have gotten away from them and they just haven't made it home yet. But until we know more...I am sure they are all right," he said trying to comfort me and helping to take my worries away.

"I bet you might be just a little hungry and if it is okay with you I'll take you to town and my wife can clean you up and fix you a good hot meal."

"But I need to be here when they come home," I cried knowing that the thought of my empty stomach and a good meal was very tempting. I was so empty down deep in my stomach that any food would be a relief.

"I'll tell you what, I will leave them a note that you are with me and they can come to town to pick you up. How will that be?'

"Well... I guess that would be okay. Can I take Little Tom with us?"

"Who is Little Tom? I thought you were all alone."

"Little Tom is my pet cat Ma and Pa gave me for Christmas."

"Aa hu... well I guess in that case, I think we better take Little Tom with us too."

"You better say that Little Tom is with us too on the note so my parents won't worry about the cat," I said.

Chapter II

In the early morning hours just after sunrise and just before the wild birds began searching for food, Martin Roth came across the decomposing body of a white man. Roth, was a kind of beach bum who gathered drift wood that was washed ashore after a storm. Martin Roth was in his late fifties and came to Florida after losing his job in a furniture factory up north. Roth was unclean with lengthy bushy hair and a long beard. Being single and not being able to find a job in south Florida, he developed a skill of making folk art furniture out of the drift wood that he collected along the beaches. Today he found more than he wanted.

His search took him to the edge of beach where the water pushed a good deal of debris and drift wood, and today a human body.

Martin wasn't shocked by the sight of dead bodies because he helped pull drowned victims from the mud after a terrific storm flooded the town he was living in, but this wasn't Tennessee and he really wasn't expecting to find a body here. The flies were already swarming and crabs started having their way with dead things, and it was just a matter of time before the buzzards would start forming on the dead body. He took out his handkerchief and tied it over his nose and mouth to help cut down on the smell, and then made the sign of the cross on himself and looked closer at the body. It was a body of what looked like a male about his mid to late twenties but the size was somewhat distorted by the way the body was bloated and all twisted up. The corpse lay on its side so Martin reached down and turned the stiff body over. He thought that he might be able to recognize who it might be because he thought he knew almost everybody in these parts. The man wasn't anybody that he recognized. The mans eyes were open and as Martin's finger touched the eyelids to pull them forward he saw the vision of the gray empty sea staring back at him. He pulled the skin over the eyes and the hair on his arms stood on edge and a ice cold chill fell over him even in the ninety degree heat. It was hard enough to tolerate the smell so he didn't want to go poking into the mans pockets for any identification. As he was standing over the deceased man he noticed farther down the beach what looked like another form of a human body.

Roth went to the other corpse and noticed a sea gull picking at what looked like a bright red ribbon tied to the hair of the body. This person appeared to be a girl but it was hard to tell the age because of the degree of deterioration. He thought to himself, "Thank God her eyes are closed," he didn't want to go though that experience again. The body was much smaller and Martin Roth thought he could move it over to the other by himself. He pulled a rubber poncho out of his back-pack, rolled the small body of the girl onto the poncho and dragged it back trying to not damage the corpse in the process as he went. After placing the body next to the other he tried to wipe off the sand that collected on his sweat soaked arms hoping that would take away some of the smell that attached to him. It was hard to believe that not to long ago these two poor souls were warm vibrant people that had their whole life ahead of them. Now nothing left but a couple of festering bloated carcasses with such a nauseating smell that it was hard to comprehend. He then took a couple of steps up wind and took a strong breath of salt air to try to clear his nose of the disgusting stench.

"Damned," he muttered to himself' staring down at the two distended bodies and shaking his head. "God-A-Mighty, God-A-Mighty," he whispered shaking his head back and forth. It was as close as he could come to saying a prayer.

Martin tried to cover the two deceased people with the poncho and then stacked some palm fronds and debris over them so that the buzzards could not readily get to them. Thinking they would be okay for a short time he made the lengthy trip back to town and reported what he found to sheriff Pool. Pool asked Martin Roth to go get Moses and a wagon team of mules from the county stable to bring back the bodies.

"Lordy what done happen to des poo folk?" Moses said as he dipped a rag in the water and tied it over his mouth.

By now the heat of the sun, the damage from the salt water and the small creatures continuing their destruction to the bodies, was making a bad situation even more horrible.

Sheriff Pool said, “We’ll figure that after we get them back to town. Go get the treated tarps and we’ll try to roll them up in them to hold down the smell.

“My God... this one looks like she is just a young girl,” Pool said looking at the female body.

The men tried to get all of the bright little crabs off the decaying bodies and rolled them onto the rubber like tarps and carried them to the wagon. The smell was so strong they felt it was going to take a heap of scrubbing to get it out of their skin pores. They handled the bodies with utmost respect and dignity, but as they lifted the larger body into the back of the wagon the mule team jerked, pulled forward and Moses was caught holding the whole load.

Martin now sitting at the front of the wagon dropped the straps to the mules and had to jump down, and grab the halter to gentle the team down.

Once the bodies were secured in the wagon, Martin said to Sheriff Pool, “If it is all right wit you I’ll just stay here and finish what I was doing. I spent too much of this day not makin any money already.”

“Sure that’s okay, beside I know where I can find you if I need you, besides I am sure you didn‘t have anything to do with this. Come on Mose let's get back to town and find out who these people are. Maybe they have something to do with that boat Tom found yesterday."

They took their unpleasant load to Dr. Walker to be examined and maybe be identified. The seventy-two year old Dr. Mason Walker was the only doctor in Buzzard Bay and he also substituted as the local funeral director. In examining the two deceased he determined that they died by drowning and that they did not have any identification on them. The only thing that he found was a one inch paint brush in the pocket of the man's bib-overalls.

When the process was finished the doctor walked over to the sheriffs office and asked," Should I order a couple of pine boxes from Boxer's store?"

"Yes sir, I guess so. And you say you didn't find any identification on either one of them?"

"No, just that little paint brush on the feller."

The sheriff scratched his head and said, "Well I guess I could take a photo of them and take it around town to see if anybody recognized them. After all Buzzard ain't that big that they wouldn't be recognized right off the bat. But in the mean time get Leon started on them pine boxes."

Leon Boxer got in touch with Martin Roth because he built cabinets for him from time to time and of course there wasn't much difference in a pine box than in a cabinet. It only took Martin a couple of hours to get the job done and when he and Leon delivered the coffins; Leon caught a glimpse of Hector on a table in the other

room.

"My Good Lord... what has happened to Hector? Is this who we been makin these boxes fer?"

"Do you know this man and woman?" said Doc Walker.

"Woman?... ohoo-o-o nooo-o-o... not that sweet little gal too? What has happened to them? The boy? Where is the boy? Is the boy here too?"

"What boy? What are you talkin bout? I never saw a boy and I'm the one that found them," said Martin. "I didn't see no boy and I looked all over the shore to see if there was a boat or anything else."

"This man is Hector Dalton and his wife Grace Dalton and they have a young boy by the name of Timmy. I think that is the boy's name," said Leon.

"Martin, go over and tell the sheriff that Leon knows who these poor folk are," said Dr. Walker. "And don't forget to tell him that there is a boy somewhere out there too."

****

Mrs. Freda Pool was a very kind person but not too

pretty. She was overweight and unappealing with stringy oily dark brown hair and had some kind of a blotchy skin problem. But what she lacked in looks she made up for in having a very motherly like personality and also being a great cook. The Pool's didn't have any children but they really knew how to take care of children.

I must have eaten enough for two people but I guess I was just making up for the last three days. Then Mrs. Pool insisted on me taking a bath and get cleaned up while she washed my clothes. I never took a bath in a real bathtub inside of a house before and it sure felt good. Then she gave me one of Mr. Pool's oversized work shirts to put on and I lay down on the sofa while she dried my cloths by the kitchen stove. I fell asleep within minutes from exhaustion with Little Tom curled up beside me.

The next day about noon I was awakened to the sounds of men talking in the kitchen. I dressed in my clean clothes that lay on a chair beside me and moved closer to the kitchen door so I could hear what they were saying.

"It's goin to be pretty dern hard tellin the boy that the two bloated, crab picked bodies that I found in the tangled thicket down on the bay were his Ma and Pa."

Time seemed to stop... then rushed forward to what I just heard. I was sure they weren't talking about *my* Ma and Pa. And maybe I really didn't hear him right at that. There was no way that it was my parents because they were going to come home any time now and then we will all be together again. Life will be just like it was before the storm and it will just be a bad dream.

"No, not my parents," I cried deep inside. *"Not my parents."*

The rough looking man that was talking to Mr. Pool said while stroking his long gray beard, "I sure wouldn't want to be in y'all shoes when y'all tell the kid."

"Kin I pour another cup of coffee?" he said, with words that flowed without any concern about the serious discussion that he just had.

"Well it isn't your job, but I don't want to do it either. Maybe I can get Freda to sit down with him and break the news to him," the policeman said.

"My wife is a whole lot more comforting than I am when it comes to things like this."

"Y'all want any of this?" the scruffy man said setting the coffee pot down on the stove.

I wanted to run out of the house but my legs were paralyzed and I couldn't get them to move. I couldn't see because my eyes were full of tears and I couldn't think because my mind went black. So black that there was no spark of thought left inside.

Just then Mrs. Pool saw me, "Oh no; the boy overheard you big lugs."

"Oh brother what have I've done? The older I get the bigger my mouth gets, and before to long I should be able to get my whole foot in my mouth without too much trouble," said Martin Roth with distress in his voice.

"I can't believe you insensitive men could say them words around the boy. There ain't nothing opened more by mistake than the mouth. Come here boy," Mrs. Pool said as she walked toward me.

She touched my hand and I melted as she drew me closer to her.

I thought that if I closed my eyes and kept them closed, today will all go away. With my eyes shut tight I could see my parents clearly... we are happy... and nothing ever happened.

She sat down and said, "Come to me child and sit on my lap; I have some terrible, terrible news to tell you."

Oh God... the God I knew would never let something like this come to pass.

"Timmy, open your eyes and look at me... everything will be all right," said Mrs. Pool.

I wanted to keep my eyes closed... stay this way... in the dark it was more peace-full than in the light and I was with my family.

I sat with her but I couldn't hear anything she was saying. My body was there but my mind was shut off and somewhere else. Maybe I didn't want to hear, I didn't want to believe anything she said. She held me close and kept trying to tell me that in time my pain will heal.

"Please open your eyes and listen to me . We will be here for you and take care of you."

Chester Pool put his hand on his wife's shoulder and said, "Don't promise the boy anything that we might not be able to keep."

Eyes still closed and I am with my Ma and Pa... and I am not this sad little boy anymore.

"Do you understand what I just said?"

I imagined her mouth moving but nothing coming out. I just sat there... my face was cold and wet with tears.

"You can stay here with us for a few days or at least until we find out if you have anybody that you can go to live with," said the policeman with a mixed professional coolness in his voice.

Again just the mouth moving but no sound coming out. Hand gestures, bodies moving across the room. Nothing.

Without any intention my body began to shake and my skin turned whiter than normal with a cold sweat.

"Is he okay, Freda? He has an emptiness in his face that I have never seen in a person before."

"I think so, just in some kind of shock," she said.

Just then as if an animal can tell that something terrible is wrong, Little Tom jumped on my lap between me and Mrs. Pool and began to lick the tears from my face. I opened my eyes and my heart began to beat in a normal way again. I pulled the small black cat closer to me and I felt that I had to console him instead of feeling sorry for myself.

Bringing me closer to her warmth and trying to help me understand what has happened Freda Pool said, "You don't have to think about anything right now, Timmy. You are more than welcome to stay with us for as long as it takes. I am amazed you are taking all this unpleasant happening just like a big grown up man."

Chapter 12

"Precious Lord , take my hand, take me on to the land..." sang three people standing by the grave site along with the preacher saying, "The Lord is my shepherd: I shall not want. He maketh me to lie down in green pastures:"

I never heard those words before but they along with the singing was soothing to me.

"He leadeth me beside still waters," the minister continued.

The cemetery was about a half mile out of town next to a pleasant scenic little spring fed pond with crystal clear water. Several giant oak trees that were shading the burial spots had long streams of Spanish moss gently waving in the air. It was an old cemetery going back to the Civil War, with several of the uncared for grave sights sunken in, and with most grave markers too hard to read the names on them. The sun was already scorching hot at 10 o'clock in the morning but there was a pleasant breeze blowing a fragrant smell of wild oranges blooming that filled the air. They placed my father in a plain pine wooden box in a deep hole and directly on top of him they placed my mother's box so they were together in one grave site. This was not uncommon in this part of Florida and at this time, especially if two people of the same family died at the same time. A single grave plot was donated by funds raised by the towns people. The funeral ceremony was conducted by the Reverend Morris Wright of the Southern Baptist Church and attendees were Mr. Star, Miss Penelope Jones, Mr. and Mrs. Pool and even Leon S. Boxer from the hardware store. There were three other people that stood by the Reverend Wright that I did not know. My heart was broken and I was very much alone even with all these strangers around me while they sang strange hymns of which I did not know any of the words or quite understand their meaning.

"Ashes to ashes, dust to dust," continued the somber preacher.

Suddenly I was jarred by the strange spine-chilling

sound that is made by a mourning dove when it takes flight. I wanted so dreadfully to see my parents for one last time so that I could say my goodbye's face to face but they already had the coffins closed and nailed shut when I got to the cemetery.

Reverend Wright looked my way and I felt that he was speaking just to me when he said, "When you die... well sir, our body is just a physical home for your soul. You should not worry what is done with what is left of your remains. Your spirit and soul are one in the same and they are still present when your physical body is in a room or not, live or dead."

He rubbed his head and wiped the sweat from his face and went on, "You see your body is just a resting place until you die. At that time your soul is set free and your spirit is felt by many people in many places at various times."

I remember those words as if I was hearing them today but at that time I didn't know what they meant. I just felt the dark and emptiness in me.

"Always remember that your parents will be with you no matter where you are," he said.

I moved closer to the fissure in the ground that was to

be where my parents were going to be entombed, and as I looked into the hole, I thought I could feel the strong presence of my parents. The sweet smell of my mother's hair as she dried it in the warm summer sun. The intoxicating smells of oil paint and turpentine on my Pa's hands as he worked on his signs. Almost to the point that they were going to come out of the ground and greet me... and tell me this has all been just a dreadful dream. But no... this wasn't going to happen, and I had to face the reality that I will never see them again. *I thought to myself... do you sleep in peace and will you be cold tonight?*

The preacher closed his book and people started walking away once they could see the service was concluded. A large strange looking man came over to fill in the grave as I watched. The man was white... I thought, but with all the features of a black man. Large broad nose and thick round lips and had a kind of kinky off colored yellow hair. He grabbed his shovel and with the first shovel full of dirt that landed directly on top of my parents I screamed out, "Ma-m-a!" Birds flew out of the tree branches and small ground animals ran for cover from my cry. "Pa-pa don't leave me alone," I continued to cry.

My thought at this point was to jump in on top of the soft -pine boxes and let him cover me over too.

The strange man stopped what he was doing for a second and looked directly into my eyes, but never said a word. His pale gray-blue eyes burned deep into my brain. He reached out and touched me on the shoulder and at that instant I felt some strange form of comfort. When the odd looking man was finished with his job, policeman Pool told him to go get into his police car and they left to go back to town.

I wanted to stay by their grave even after my parents were covered over, but eventually I was pulled away by Mrs. Pool and we went back to town with her friends.

I missed my parents with a hurt that was unbearable. The soft touch of my mother's gentle hand on me is still felt today and I can in spite of everything see my father showing me how to paint. Maybe that is what the preacher was talking about. I was holding Little Tom close to me and trying to put my state of mind together as to how this chapter in my life was going to play out. I fell deep into myself and even stopped talking when confronted by people. Mrs. Pool began to worry about me and began to spend more time with me trying to coax me to speak to her.

I was with the Pool family for three days and I wanted to go home where I used to live and be with my pets and where I was more familiar. There was talk from the policeman that my mother had a father that was thought to be still alive and lived somewhere in the Seminole State Park area. Mr. Pool was trying to locate him to tell him that he had a grandson. I also overheard him and Freda having a conversation that if he couldn't locate my Grand Pa, he was going to take me to the county orphanage. With great passion Mrs. Pool objected to this idea. But I suspected that the town policeman was the boss in this family and I didn't want to think of the suggestion of going to an orphanage. Nor was I interested in living with a person that I never met, no matter who he was. I just wanted to take Little Tom and go home. I wanted my Ma and Pa and everything to be the way it was. I wanted my life back the way it was before this nightmare began.

My parents were not of any one faith but they did teach me that there was a God that created all of us and all of the wonders of the world and that he watched over us to make sure that nothing bad happened to us. How could there be a God like that, that would do this to me. I did not believe there is a God... at least not one that was watching over me. This day, at this time I made a decision that there wasn't anybody looking after me and I was going to have to be the only one to take care of myself.

I was back in school and everybody treated me oddly. They acted as if it was my fault that my parents perished in the storm. Miss Jones did try to give me a little more attention when she could. On the fourth day walking to the Pool's house from school, I was passing the bus station where the bus driver was loading some boxes and luggage into the side of the bus. I thought to myself that this would be a good way for me to escape. Maybe if I could hide in the bus and ride to the next town I would be on my own and I could take care of myself. I waited for the driver to go into the building and I climbed into the side of the bus and pulled a large suit-case in front of me. The only thing I was sorry about was that I didn't have Little Tom with me, but this was a possibility to get away and I had to take the chance. Just when I thought I was on my way, a strange rough hand grabbed my arm and pulled me out of the bus.

"Hey... what are you doing," I cried out.

"Boy yus better not be in dar," the stranger said.

The man was the odd looking white person that worked on the grave at the cemetery. He scared me half to death but he was soft spoken and gentle, and that brought an air of peace within me.

"Come with me, boy, b'for somebody sees us round dis cheer bus."

I walked with him to a bench on the other side of the street and we sat down.

"Why did you stop me from hiding on the bus? I said somewhat aggravated.

"Boy, don't yus know ya kin get hurt playing round like dat. What if da driver woulda closed da door and drove away with yus in thar?"

"That's what I wanted to do, you big dummy. I was trying to run away from here."

The strange man looked around to see if anybody was coming and said, "It's pretty tough to be on yore own at yus age. Take my word fer it, cause I knows what I am talkin bout."

"How would you know?" I said, still upset that he stopped me.

"Boy, I knows," the man said. "I knows."

"Why yus want to git outa cheer so bad? Don't da Boss takes good care of yus?

I wondered who was this man and how did he know so much about me and why did he even care.

"Why do you care?"

"Boss Pool done told me bout yus, and I feels bad fo ya, but ya need to stay where ya is. Dem people is good people and day gona take good care of ya."

After telling him that I heard Mr. Pool was going to put me in an orphanage if they couldn't find any relatives to take me in he said, "Just stay where ya is and all is gona be okay. Yus just too young to be on ya own."

He walked most of the way to the Pool's house to

make sure that I wouldn't try to run away, but I still had it in the back of my mind that some how I was going to go off on my own just as soon as I could.

Late the evening of the next day, I stuffed my pockets with what food I found in the kitchen and snuck out of the house and with Little Tom and made my way back to the shack were we used to live. I was about to commit my fate with all my Christian reservation. When I came to the shack I found somebody must have come by and took my pets or maybe turned them loose.

I spent the rest of the night there and I could feel the presence of my Ma and Pa at every glance I took and in everything that I touched. I could smell my Mother cooking grits over the stove and for a split fading moment I

could see my Father working on a sign for old Leon. I found the note that Chester Pool left for my parents on the table and put it into my pocket. I was home... but I decided that in the morning I better not stay too long because this would be the first place they would come to look for me. I gathered what items that meant something to me and put them into a pillowcase. After unsuccessfully searching for some time for the photo of my parents and started on my new journey, maybe I will head for the land where the Seminole Indians live. Maybe I could be taken in and be raised by the Indians.

I managed to go a good distance from the shack by that evening and found myself at the edge of a vast swamp. I was exhausted and didn't want to go any further because night was coming on.

The night was most terrifying. I slumbered in a hollowed out log unable to completely enter the world of unconsciousness. Every noise was magnified a hundred times over making me think that any minute I would be attacked by some strange and menacing monster. Even the smallest insect crawling on the log made the hair stand up on my arms. It was an uncommonly warm night but I was chilled to the bone and I used every bit of clothing that I brought with me to try and stay warm. As the black monster of night crept in, and the light of day melted away, I reached out to grab onto anything to keep from sliding back into the cold damp void of my mind. The madness with its claw like fingers dug hard into my shoulder and held me there in suspension until I fell into a numb slumber.

The next morning the first rays of the sun forced its light out into the dark hammock and punched holes through the trees, I could hear voices in the distance hollering out my name.

"Timmy where are you," the voices called out.

"Where are you boy, we came to take you home where you will be safe," they called out again.

I was safe when I was with my Ma and Pa but I didn't feel that I was safe with these people. I have to protect myself and keep out of harm's way to take care of myself... nobody else could do that. They will not find me, not where I am going. I got up and headed into the swamp away from the voices and into more danger.

"Timmy," the voices got softer the farther I moved.

****

Moses "Mose" Blue-eyed Cat, an outcast son of descendents of southern slaves, was a prisoner of officer Pool. He was arrested and serving time for stealing food from the grocery store and resisting arrest which earned him sixty days in the poky. Mose as I said was an outcast because he was a freak of nature, he was an albino person. Not just an albino, but a Negro albino. That is a pale all white-skinned, gray-blue eyed, blond kinky hair, black person. The color of his skin made a difficult situation for him from the day he was born.

It was a hard birth that lasted twelve hours of the evening and into the early morning. A terrible storm raged through the night. Moses was born and almost immediately was placed into the arms of the black mother.

She screamed and cried out to her husband, "Take dis unholy thing and get rid of it."

When the father held up the child in the candle light he too started to tremble, "What sins have we done that we gived birth to a monster like dis?"

The frightened parents wanted to kill him because they thought he was a bad demon and if he lived he would bring very bad fortune to them. But a Seminole

Indian woman that helped with the birthing agreed to take the baby to raise as her own, not thinking of what she was getting herself into. Being a Indian woman that wasn't married, she took the child back to the Indian village for help in raising the strange white boy.

By the age of ten "Blue-Eyed Cat" the name the Indian woman gave him, was too much to handle and the Seminole Indian couldn't control him anymore so he was put out on his own.

He tried to fit in with the whites in several towns but they turned their backs to him too, because they thought he was a freak and nobody wanted him around.

The next few years were not easy for Moses but somehow he survived and grew to be a large strapping man. He was constantly in trouble, in and out of one jail or another. Nothing too serious, just enough to get thirty to forty days of jail time. Or you can look at it in this way, thirty to forty days of free food and a clean bed to sleep on.

At this time he only had a few days of jail time left and Moses had grown very found of Freda Pool's good old home cooking so he decided to take off from the street cleanup job that officer Pool put him on. He knew that Chester Pool was a pretty good tracker and he would be back in jail for another thirty days and the good food in no time what-so-ever. So Blue-Eyed-Cat just walked away and went into the backwater swamp knowing that would be the first place the cop would look for him. The only thing he didn't know that Chester Pool was heading up a search party for a frightened little boy that probably went home, to the shack where he lived with his parents before they were buried in the grave that Moses had opened and then closed.

Chapter 13

The vast great swamp wasn't too bad to start with but as the day progressed the saw grass grew taller and more hostile. At times, I felt that I was in a giant puzzle. Water at times was almost to my shoulders where Little Tom rode, but I went on. Finally about noon, just beyond a very high growth of saw grass, I came to a section of high ground with one very tall oak tree and several small shade trees where I stopped to rest and dry off. My hands and face had a number of small cuts from the saw grass and my shoes were full of mud. I found and removed several unusual looking bugs on various parts of my body and rubbed the spots with mud.

I found a bush full of wild berries like the ones my mother used to make pies with so I ate my fill of them and saved my oranges for later. So far I think I was doing a pretty fair job of taking care of myself. I thought for sure I didn't need anybody to take me under their wing, not even God. After stuffing myself with the berries I sprawled out under the cool shade of the oak tree closed my eyes and dosed off.

A vibrant red rat snake slithering across my chest startled me to be awake. I knew he was harmless and other than being aroused, I wasn't afraid. The temperature dropped about ten degrees as the sky formed dark ominous gray clouds with the afternoon showers that were about to come. There was thunder off in the distance from a heat storm but no signs of anything more than a shower here. I felt that I traveled far enough for the day anyway so I picked some more berries and caught a few crayfish to feed Little Tom and sat back to wait for the rain to stop. I made a bed under the large oak tree with some leaves and strips of palms and curled up with Little Tom to try to fall asleep again. Except for a few irritating small cuts and a empty spot in my belly, I thought I was doing pretty good for myself.

That night was much better than the first, and I was so exhausted that it didn't take much for me to fall to sleep.

I was startled awake the next morning by an acorn shell falling on my head from a squirrel having breakfast far above me in the oak tree and soon I was on my way again. I walked as far as I could go before I had to get back in the water. The route I took was scattered with small hammocks so I just moved from one patch of land to another. By mid day I wandered onto a stretch of land that seemed to go on for a long way.

At a slow pace walking along the path I found a stand of wild banana plants. I sat on a large mound of dirt and ate until my belly was full. Little Tom found a nice fat field mouse and he ate his fill too. Then in the shade of the banana plants I found a comfortable place to take a late afternoon nap and with Little Tom by my side... dozed off.

"You give me money you has, old man!"

"I kill you old man, if you don't gives me what money you has!"

Old man... did I hear something or was I just dreaming? My eyes were closed so I figured I must be just dreaming. I didn't understand what it was that I was dreaming, but it seemed so real. Why would I dream about an old man? I just couldn't figure it out.

"I no wait any mo' old man, the money... or I kill you!"

The voice was much louder this time as I tried to open my eyes. I could not understand, *old man... money*? I don't have any money, except my shinny silver dollar. I forced my one eye open and tried to focus about me to see if I was dreaming. I could not see anything from were I was and I still thought I was just dreaming. But I just couldn't figure out what the voice meant...*old man.* Little Tom didn't move either so I must have just thought it was in my mind.

"I aint' gots no money, and beside if'n I did, ya be the last pecker wood that would git it from me."

Woo... that was really loud and clear and I knew that I must have been hearing all these words. I sat up, eyes wide open now, and my center of attention brought me to a clearing in the road where I could see a man that looked like a colorful dressed Seminole Indian with a knife pointing it at an old white man with a large palm frond hat and an eagles feather tucked in it.

"Hey you!" I yelled erupting my voice as loud as I could.

My squeaky young voice wasn't enough to scare anybody but it was enough of a screech to startle the Indian for a split second so that the old man could get his firearm out of his holster and point it at the Indian.

"Now ya git ya red skin out of cheer b'for I put a big hole in ya."

Then he fired his firearm into the air and with the loud noise, the Indian dropped his knife an turned tail and ran toward me with utmost speed.

I was so scared that I jumped off the road into the water while Little Tom ran into the bushes. The Indian ran by me at a fast speed and didn't look to see who I was or where I was because he was so terrified that he was going to be shot by the old man with his next shot. When I looked up the tanned wrinkled man was standing over the spot that I dove into the water and was rearranging his pistol back into his belt.

He looked down at me and holding out his hand he said, "Boy ya kin come out of thar now. I do not believe that skin will be back in dis parts gin, thanks to ya. That was mighty brave of ya."

"I was just waitin for a time that I could get the drop on that low life and ya gived me that chance. I am in ya favor, thank ya."

Shaking my hand until I thought it would fall off he said, " What ya doin a way out cheer, boy?"

Somehow I felt that I could trust this kindly old man and I answered, " It is a long story, but the truth is my Ma and Pa has been killed in a storm, and I am running away from the people that was taking care of me."

"Where ya from? I got some food if'n ya hungry."

"I am from a place near Buzzard Bay in Collier county. That is where I lived with my Ma and Pa and Little Tom. Come to think of it, where is that little fellow?"

Looking around the old man said, "Whos dis Little Tom ya said, I don't see nobody?"

Just then out came Little Tom from his hiding place and I said, "There he is. Little Tom is my cat... my Ma and Pa gave to me last Christmas."

Laughing at the sight of the little black ball, the old man picked him up and said, "Ya is quite the little critter, ain't ya?"

We sat and talked while the old man built a fire and fixed some fish that he caught earlier with biscuits that tasted surprising like my Ma made.

Chapter 14

We sat and talked for what seemed like hours while skeeters and night bugs started to swarm around us.

I noticed he had a large pile of beaver pelts and rolled up gator skins. He explained that he was a gator hunter and also trapped beaver and other critters for their pelts and sold them in the nearby town. He hadn't sold his skins and pelts yet so he didn't have any money to give the Indian anyway. That is where he was going when he was stopped by the Indian robber. This was his way of life. A way of life that seemed to me to be hard and very lonely. He also told me he had a cabin about a mile down the road... back in a stand of oaks and pines that was impossible to see from the road. He also let me know that nobody ever saw his cabin or knew were he lived except his old Indian woman friend that would help him with the skins.

"Boy ya got a knife?"

I didn't have any weapons and I didn't quite know what he was meaning by the question but I stuttered back, "No sir, I don't have any weapons."

"Well cheer ya kin take dis un... ya earned it. If'n ya goin be on yer own out cheer, ya goin need sumpun to keep ya out of harm. Thar be lot o' bad critters in the wilderness."

It was the knife that the Indian had and the old man was giving it to me. I never owned a knife before, not that my parents were against knives, but they said that I had no need for one. This knife was beautiful. Wow...wee was it beautiful! It was hand made with a deer antler for the handle and thin leather strips with brilliant colorful beads tied tightly around the handle to make up the grip. The steel blade was brightly polished and was honed to a extremely sharp edge and I could even see my dirty face in the blade. It didn't have a sheaf to carry it in because that was probably still on the Indians belt, but I thought that I could make one for it myself later on. I thought it must be very valuable and I was sure the Indian was going to miss it.

"Thank you sir, but don't you think the Indian will be back to try to get his knife from me?" I said, not wanting any trouble with the Red Skin.

"Na boy, ya don't have to worry none bout that skin. He's probably half way cross the state by now and thankin his Injun maker that I didn't plug him."

The trapper didn't ask much about me or my parents so... I didn't contribute that information. He told me his name was Mar Sands and I told him my name was Timothy and I didn't give my last name not knowing if I could trust him yet. I could not help but notice that his hat was made much in the same manner of the way my mother made her hats, but I didn't mention the similarity.

"Boy it's gettin late an we best be gettin to da cabin," as he kicked the fire out and packed up what was left of the food.

I hesitated not knowing what to do so I just stood there looking at Mar.

"Common boy? I ain't gonna skine ya, I don't think thars any money in boy skins."

He had a loud bull frog type of laugh and said as he slapped his legs, "At least I don't thin they is."

I thought that I could take care of myself out on the road but it sure would be nice to sleep in a real bed to-night. There was some kind of bond that I was beginning to feel toward this old man and thought that I could take a chance on him. There was just something about him... I just couldn't figure it out.

Picking up Little Tom I ask, "Can I bring my cat with me?"

"Sure boy, he kin play with my squirrels that runs in an out of da cabin."

We arrived at a shoddy crude cabin, built up from what looked like left over odds and ends of other torn down shacks and I could see the man truly lived alone. I could see inside with the moon-light the cabin was very cluttered, dirty and dark with only one window in the front by the door and more skins scattered about. The floor was just dirt with a few boards laid around to stand on when if it rained hard and the water would come in. There was a mattress that was stuffed with dried moss on a cot in the corner at the highest part of the floor. A home made table with two chairs that did not match sat in the center of the room and a large wooden chest sat on some boards with more skins piled on it at the opposite wall. There was no sink and no stove in the cabin. All of the cooking and washing took place outside. More skins were stretched out on the side of the building outside. The cabin had a musty odor of death about it but I still felt relaxed here and I had no fear of the old man that took me in.

Mar Sands looked like a man that lived in the swamps all his life and by his dark tanned wrinkled skin it looked like he had it pretty rough. He wore faded blue bib-overalls with the legs tucked into black muddy boots that came up to his knees. He was without a shirt, just a crude gator skin vest that was tied shut with pieces of deer skin strips. Surprisingly Mar did not carry the smell that came from the skins that he handled, he just didn't have any smell to him at all. Nor did he have any of the body odor that you would expect from a person that lived in the wild and worked as hard as he did. He did not smoke or chew but he did chew on a small stick all of the time and rarely took it out of his mouth except when he ate. His long white hair was left unruly and hidden under his hat that he hardly ever took off. He did have a short beard that he said he shaved off at least once a month. He said that he could judge when a month was over by how much his beard grew.

Along with his revolver he carried his own kind of knife. A formable blade with no frills that I guessed to be about ten inches in length and was strapped to his belt. He also had a deer skin whip with a wood handle that was coiled and fastened to his belt along with a deer skin pouch. The whip was the typical type of whip that was used by the Florida cow-hands that were called Crackers because of the sound that was made by the whip when used to bring in the cattle. I felt that the old man was well versed in the use of all his weapons but did not flaunt his knowledge.

"Boy ya kin bed on the cot tonight caus I liks to sleep outside this time of da year."

And then he went outside and I did not see him again until the next morning.

"Thank you sir," and I bid him a good night.

I moved some pelts off from the wooden cot, straightened up an aged rough wool blanket, and Little Tom and I fell asleep as soon as we lay back on the cot. My dreams that night were the first peaceful dreams that I had since my parents died.

Chapter 15

The sun nudged hot sparks of light through the doorway helping me to wake up. I could hear turtle doves cooing in the tall pine trees around the cabin. I rubbed my eyes and tried to put together where I was. Slowly Little Tom stood up stretched, and with his mouth wide open, yawned. Now slowly memories of events from yesterday started to settle in my brain like a squirrel stowing acorns away for the winter. Nothing bad for a change. My scratches and bumps seemed to have melted away and I felt well rested.

Sweet smells of fat-back frying over an open fire along with hot cakes streaming into the grimy cabin made me excited to be alive and very hungry.

Two bodies were slumped over large tree stumps near the open fire where the fat bacon drippings sputtered on the open coals.

"You think Charley Black Bear come back to rob you gin?" The strange voice came from where the fire pit blazed.

"Naw, he ain't got brains but he's got the fear of my revolver in him," the old man said.

"Pass the coffee, I ain't wake yet."

"You try goin to town today, cus I used last of flour in flat cakes."

I could hear another voice beside Mr. Sands and I walked toward the door to see who the stranger was. The unfamiliar person was an elderly Indian woman sitting by the fire, wrapped in a very colorful blanket with a multitude of vibrant broad stripes. She wore her hairstyle with long bangs and a tight bun in the back with large eagles' feathers fastened in it. I later learned that Seminole women only let their hair down in times of personal mourning. Large strands of very colorful beads adorned her neck and with the way the blanket wrapped around her I could see that she was of small structure.

"Com n' boy, bout time yus up, it's almost six." Sands called to me.

"Sit cheer by me and git some grub," he said moving

over a smidge.

As he moved over to make room for me he introduced me to the Indian, " Dis cheer is my friend Ghost Swamp Flower."

The old woman turned to me and just made a grunting noise. Her skin was a donut crusty brown complexion and her dark eyes were sunken in.

I nodded back to her and said, "How do you do, Ma'am?"

Sands slapped his knee and grunted a spirited laugh and said, "Boy's got manners, ain't he? " said Mr. Sands.

"Uhh."

I grabbed a metal plate and introduced my stomach to a glorious stack of hot cakes and fat back.

"Boys got appetite too, ain't he?"

"Uhh," repeated the elderly Indian woman.

"May I give Little Tom a small piece of fat back, Sir?"

"Sure ya kin, but don't calls me sir. Just calls me Mar."

"Yes Sir... I mean Mar?"

"Ya more than welcome to stays cheer with me if'n ya wants to, or til ya decide what ya wants to do, but yus got plenty o'time to figger out what ya wants."

"I would like to stay with you here for a time, at least until I can figure why God has taken my parents from me and ruined my life."

Mr. Sands, after a long conversation with me said, "I noticed that ya seem to have a lot of mean hostility cooped up in ya because of what happened to yore Ma and Pa. Ya feel that it's everybody's fault and ya even blame God."

"I am all alone and have no family or friends and I can't trust anybody, not even God, if there is one," I said with a frown on my face.

"Sit here... I have to git something out of da cabin," and the old man went to the cabin.

When he returned he had a tin can full of rusty nails along with an old hammer and said, "This is fer ya."

I looked at him with a great puzzlement, and questioned what I was to do with them.

"I would like yus to do supun fer me."

"Since you have been so kind to me, I will try to do what ever you want me to do."

The old man had me walk over to a partial fence that he stretched hides over and said, "When ever ya get dis feelin that ya blam everbody and especially God fer what ever happened to ya, I wants ya to hammer a nail into dis fence. Can ya do dis?"

"Yes sir, ah Mar, but I don't understand why you want me to do this."

Mr. Sands said that this was something he did years ago to control his temper and pain when he lost most of his family and he too blamed everybody and even God for it too. He said that believe it or not it worked.

The first day I was out by the fence bright and early, almost before the sun began to rise, driving nails all over that old fence, one after another. At times when I was really felling sorry for myself and wanted to have a pity party, I drove three and four of those rusty nails at a time. I would even have to straighten some of the bent nails because I was running out of nails to hammer into the wooden fence. Then some-

thing happened while I was unbending a really curved nail... I realized that my Ma and Pa weren't to blame for what has happened to me. And I shouldn't blame Sheriff Pool and his wife for what happened to me, after all they were just being kind to take care of me. And as far as that goes, I couldn't find anyone that I could put the blame on except maybe... God! I thought about that for a long time. After two days, I only put a nail in the fence only a couple of times and by that night I stopped all together. I did not know that much about God but I couldn't think that someone as great as He was that could create all this beauty where I lived, could be responsible for what happened to me. So for now I would just call it a draw and quit feeling sorry for myself and get back to life at hand.

"Mr. Sands?" I said rubbing a small blister on my thumb created by all the hammering that I had just done.

The old man stopped what he was doing and said, "Yes Timmy, what can I do fer ya?"

"I haven't had to put a nail in the fence for a long time, now what do want me to do now?"

"That's very good Timmy, now what I want ya to do is, whenever ya have a good thought or ya praise God that ya are alive and dat ya will make the best of yore life, that now I want ya to pull one of the nails out of the fence."

And so I did this and in only one day I successfully pulled out all of the nails. I think I understood what the old man was trying to get across to me, that no matter what happens in life you have to forgive and go on with your life or you would probably turn out to be a very miserable and hateful person.

"Very good Timmy, now I wants to show ya supum," and we went over to the fence.

"Can ya see all of dem holes in the fence?"

"Yes, sir," I said rubbing another blister made by pulling all the nails out of the fence.

"Well when ya pulled out dem nails ya took away the pain dat ya caused but ya can never take away the scars that was left from yore bad thoughts. So ya have to just have good thoughts at all the time so that you don't leave any more scars behind."

My hands were sore but I thanked the old man for the very ingenious way of showing how to accept what happens to you in your life. I thought from now on I was going to try to think the best of everybody and pledge to help anybody that needed help, and most of all I would always remember my parents for how good and protective they really were to me.

On the fourth day Mar said if I wanted to go with him when he took the pelts and skins to town, that I could. Or I could stay here and get more acquainted with Ghost Swamp Flower, the Indian woman. Not that I had any concern about the old Indian woman, I already decided to go with Mr. Sands if he would ask me. He made me at ease and I started to take a liken to the old man for some reason.

We arrived at the small laid-back town of only about fifteen or so buildings, without any incident, and went to the building where Mar sold his skins. Skins and pelts lay in stacks everywhere. The setting was dingy and dirty and I could see dust flakes floating all about the room from the rays of the sun streaming through the cracks in the walls. Behind a large desk sat a very over-weight man in bib overalls and a very sweat-stained under shirt, with his feet resting upon the desk. Behind the obese man on the wall hung the longest rattle snake skin that I ever saw. It had to be at least a twenty rattle or more, I thought.

"Well I'll be... hello Mar." the man said.

"I ain't seen ya in a coons age. Heard ya got et by a big crock down in the Blue Swamp." he went on.

"Ya sure lookin good fer a dead person," the fat man said grunting as he tried to put his fat legs back on the floor.

"Rattlesnake Pass would miss ya if'n anythin would happin to ya."

Mr. Sands laughed in his huge bull frog sound, looked at the man, and said, "Ya knows that there ain't no gator growed that could et me. Sids I don't thin he would want to et me... I'm too tuff."

"Who's this big boy, Mar?"

Mar moved his palm hat back a bit and said, "This cheer boy tis a long lost kin of mine from over at Buzzard in Collier county. Name is Timmy."

"Say hello to the man, Timmy."

"Hello sir," I said in a squeaky voice.

"Got some manners, ain't he?" The fat man said laughing.

Why does everybody think it's so funny about having manners, I thought to myself.

Then I got to witness the most exciting exchange of

words in negotiations to the sale of the skins that the old man brought to town.

"I wants $1.55 fer the small skins and $2.00 fer the bigens."

"Now come on Mar, you knows that in today's market I kaint pay that kind of money," said the proprietor of the business.

Back and forth went the conversation with neither person going to give in. The haggling went on for at least forty minutes. With Mr. Sands often picking up a skin and emphasizing certain traits about the skin and explaining why he should get his price for it. Then the buyer recoiling back and telling Mr. Sands that those skins were just average and didn't rate the higher price that the old man was asking, and that he can get that quality of skins any day of the week. And then Mr. Sands throwing the skin down, pushing his large palm hat back a bit more, throwing up his strong hairy arms and saying ... "I surly don't knows where." Then instantly it was all over and the store owner was counting out the money. I didn't know who got the better end of the deal but I would put my money on Mr. Sands.

"See ya when ya kin find some skins a bit more superior than des," the fat man said sitting back down grunting a lot while repositioning his feet on the desk.

Mr. Sands said, "I'll be back when ya gets some glasses so ya can see da skins better the next time."

Walking out of the store he said, "That man gits harder to deal wit every time I coms cheer."

The first place we went after the sell of the skins was to the saloon, where the old man got a large cold beer and ordered up a large cold root-beer for me. I never had anything like that before and it sure was enjoyable and it was for sure the first time I ever been in a saloon. When we were finished with our drinks we wandered over to the dry-goods store where the haggling started all over again for the supplies that the old man wanted. There again, just when I thought the negotiating was getting pretty good... it was all over. The two contestants started to laugh and Mar paid for the goods and then insisted that he got a bag of hard stripped candy to be thrown in with the deal.

Seems, Mr. Sands liked hard stripped candy as much as I did and we indulged in the candy all the way back to the cabin.

I know he was kidding about me being a long lost

relative, but... I thought I could do a lot worse than Mr. Sands to live with. After all I had to come to the conclusion that I was an orphan and the alternative to living with Mr. Sands was living in an orphanage.

We made it back to the cabin in the swamp just before dusk and Ghost Swamp Flower had a beautiful fat turkey along with sweet taters roasting over the fire. Little Tom setting by a tree stump never looked up at me when we entered because he was happy chomping down on an enormous turkey neck.

With seconds of the delicious turkey in my belly I said, "Thank you Mr. Sands for a glorious meal and thank you Ghost Swamp Flower for preparing such a scrumptious feast."

"Boy you dunt has to call her by that long colorful Injun name ever time ya talks to the Injun."

"But what do I call her?" I questioned.

"Well, ya kin call her Ghost or Swamp Flower or jest call her what I calls her... Injun. After all she is jest an Injun ain't she.?"

"Yes but she is your friend and I think she should have more respect than just...Injun. Just like I call you Mr. Sands out of respect to you."

"I may have been stepping onto something that I should not have said, but this is the way my parents taught me," I put my head down in respect.

"Well boy, come over cheer an sit on my lap," the old man gestured to me.

"Ya kin calls Ghost Swamp Flower, by the name I calls her as my personal and only friend, an that is... Jull after my past wife. And ya kin calls me Gramps if ya wants to. I would be largely honored if'n ya would," he said.

"I think ya would be jest like what my own grandson would be if'n I knew that I had one," he went on.

"I surely would likes to have knowed yus Ma and Pa, they seems like real good people, and I bets they be right proud of ya, and I knows they is watchen over ya right now."

I put my head on his shoulder and sobbed tears of contentment and felt that if he would have me, I would love to grow up here with him and his Indian friend.

"Timmy... I would be very happy to keep ya an take care of ya an raise ya as my own grandson. An I knows that Jull, even doe she don't say much that she is da same as me."

Chapter 16

"The thing ya has to remember is that God made all kinds of critters, and I kin see ya likes all of em, but thar is pet critters an den thar is critters that man has to use fer food or skins," Gramps was trying to explain to me.

"So when we traps an kills dem critters, member God put dem here fer us to use, but use only what we can use an not anymore den dat."

"I think that I understand what you are saying but it's hard to think that way," I said.

"Growing up the way I did, I never saw any animals killed, but I did understand that meat and leather had to come from somewhere," I explained.

After all I did like chicken, turkey, venison, and meat from cows, but I didn't know if I could be the one to do the killing.

Gramps was trying to show me how to make a palm hat, but I remember a lot of how my Ma made them and he was surprised to see that I knew how to do it.

"Timmy where did ya larn how to do dat?" he said.

I explained, "My Ma used to make hats like that to sell in town to the tourists."

"She must have been a very smart woman," he said as he worked with the palm fronds.

I thought the hat was finished but the Indian woman put the finishing touch to it by putting a strip of deer skin around the band and then she put strips of skins hanging down so that I could tie it on my head if I needed to. But the best thing of all was when she took one of her large eagle feathers out of her hair and fastened it in the hat.

"Thank you very much, it is a very attractive palm hat," I said.

While Jull worked on the hat, Gramps looked through his gator skins for just the right one. Not to big and not to small, not to old and especially not to green. Then a shout with glee, he pulled out the one skin that he was looking for.

"Yes dis is da one I am looking for," he said in a ex-

cited voice. It was one of a baby gator that he found dead in the swamp on one of his hunts.

He said that he never would kill any babies because their skins weren't worth much, but they would be when they were grown up. He then took the skin and made a very ornate sheath for my Indian knife with a belt to fasten around my small waist. He then found a very soft gator skin to make a vest for me to wear to protect me from the sun. Now I looked like a minor image of Gramps, just a whole lot younger an smaller.

By the end of the week Gramps said he thought that I was ready to go on my first hunt and that we could be gone for at least two or three days. This was going to very exciting for me. My first hunt! The Indian woman made sure we had all the supplies that we were going to need early the morning that we left but she was going to stay here and get things ready for when we got back.

"It is a beautiful day dat God has made fer us... amen," Gramps said, like a little prayer. Then He checked to make sure that Jull put everything in his pack that he was going to need for up to three days.

"Woman ya done good, maybe I'll bring ya sumpun back that ya will like," he said.

At 6:00 am in the morning the day started out comfortably cool enough but by noon the sky with no clouds made the sun relentless. The perpetual twilight of the thick overhead growth was not enough shade to keep me from melting. My shirt was soaked in sweat.

Gramps stopped us by a stream sheathing with scum and algae and then took out his handkerchief, moved the algae out of the way and soaked it in the water and preceded to wrapped it around my neck.

"Now boy, when ya gets hot next time, just do what I did an it will cool ya down," he said.

Latter I tried to give the scarf back but he said to keep

it because he had another. He also showed me another trick by putting a small pebble in my mouth and suck on it, that would keep me from getting thirsty. But he cautioned me to be careful not to swallow the stone. I knew that my Ma and Pa taught me a lot but now I realized that Grandpa Sands was taking up where they left off. I still missed my parents terribly but somehow their image was starting to fade just ever so slightly. I prayed that the day would never come when I could not vision what they looked like or the good times we had together, but, I could not wait for the day that the hurt of losing them would soon come. I know that in time the memory of my early youth would fade and I would have to strain to recall what happened to me at this time in my life.

The sun shinning through the cypress trees glistened on the edge of the swamp making little sparks on top of the water and I got to see scenery that I never dreamed existed. The colors, the shapes, the birds and even the strange bugs that were everywhere. I never saw the colors of life so radiantly before and I respected what God made where we lived and I would not trade it for any other place in the world.

I thought to myself that if I only had some paint, a

brush and a board that I could paint some of these beautiful scenes that I was introduced to here in the wild. I felt these images were being buried into my mind so that I could bring them to the front later on when I got older.

Suddenly we stopped in our tracks. Mr. Sands put his hand on my shoulder and brought me closer to him.

"Stand close to me now, Timmy," Mar said as he pulled out his trusty forty caliber revolver and aimed it to the front of him.

I was curious now... wanting to know why, and said, "What do you see, Gramps?"

Gramps put his finger to his mouth to let me know not to talk. I didn't see anything and I couldn't understand if Gramps saw anything. I stretched out around the side of the old man and strained to see.

"CA-BANG."

Just then without warning, the gun went off with a great puff of black smoke and the smell of gun powder and the loud noise scared the bee-jebbers out of me.

"Got ya, ya ol rascal!" Gramps said.

When the smoke cleared I could see what it was all about. Gramps shot our first gator. He didn't look too big in the water but once we pulled him out on land I could see that he must be at least eight feet long. Gramps got him with one shot in the head and that was all it took. I was so filled with excitement that I didn't know how to feel about the killing of a critter until later. And then I remembered what Gramps told me about the critters that God made for us to use.

That first time in the deep blue swamp, Gramps shot 2 eight foot gators and 2 six foot ones. Then he showed me how to skin them. On the last reptile that was shot he even let me help him skin the gator partly by myself by using my hunting knife. I soon found out how sharp the knife really was. Gramps also told me the best part of the gator to eat was the tail just behind the real legs. I never ate gator before so I did not know what to expect.

"When we gets back to de cabin we will have Jull cook us up one of des tails and ya will love it," he told me.

Gramps said that we had such good luck today that we didn't need to stay out in the swamp overnight. So when we got everything loaded up we headed back to the cabin.

We carried the four skins and gator tails back to the cabin and Jull went to work fixing one of the tails. On the way back Gramps picked several flowers, with their roots still attached off the cypress trees that were called Ghost Orchards and gave them to the old Indian woman. She loved the flowers and showed the flat emotion that she always showed when she was happy.

Grandpa was right, the gator tail was delicious. It had a taste that was indescribable, and to this day I prefer gator tail over any other meat if I can get it.

The Indian woman showed me how to roast gator tail and many other foods. She also taught me how to weave deer skin strips and make cracker whips that she said I could sell the next time I went to town. And I showed her how to draw birds, flowers and palm trees.

"Do you really think that somebody would buy this whip from me when it's finished?" I asked Jull.

Gramps looked at the whip that I finished so far and said, "Ya, I know ya kin. Dats gona be a fine whip when ya gets done wit it."

He went on to say, "Dem cow men pays real good money fer a whip if'n the whip makes a good crack when it's worked, and I will show ya how to make a handle fer it when it's ready fer one."

Chapter 17

Like all children at my age, there are things that just drive you nuts with inquisitiveness, and the rustic chest in the cabin was a great curiosity to me. I could not escape the thought that it might contain fabulous treasures. It got to the point that at night when I would go into the cabin to go to bed, the first thing I would do was walk to the old worn out trunk and gaze at it for a few minutes, and wonder what secrets it held. The rustic historical look alone made it worthy of all of my thoughts. Should I look or should I not look? Oh I was sure the chest had many things of enormous value. After all Gramps sold a lot of skins and animal pelts, and the times I went with him to sell them, he got a good deal more money for them than he spent on supplies. So I thought there must be lots of silver coins or even gold coins in the chest. He has been living out here for years, and all those years would surely add up to a great deal of money. Beside... didn't the Indian that tried to rob Gramps think that the old man had money even before Gramps had sold his skins at the time when I first met him. Gold! Yea gold... that must be what is in the chest, lots and lots of gold.

Or maybe there was something about Mr. Sands and his undisclosed past. Something that would tell me who he really was and all about where he came from and how he came about living way out here in the swamp, secretly away from everyone. Wow... what if he is a escaped criminal and that is why he hides way out here away from the modern civilization. No, uh-ah, I couldn't believe anything like that about the kind generous man that I was living with.

"Oh... Timmy forget about that old worn out chest," I would say scolding myself, trying to get my mind from thinking about it.

I know that it wasn't any of my business of what was in the chest anyway, but there it sat... not moving... or saying anything. Just there across from me, not more than five feet away! But I could swear that I could hear a whisper from it, "Tim-m-y...! Timmy... over here! Look at me!"

Again, "Tim-m-y... why don't you come over here and sit with me? Why don't you move all these pelts off from me and take a little peek inside... just a little peek?" After all, it had no lock so it wouldn't be hard to look in it.

You would think the container would take pity on me and just fall apart and that way I wouldn't have to do anything to open it up. After all it was very old and looked like it could just come apart at the seams at any minute.

Occasionally it would take some time for me to fall asleep just thinking about that darn old chest. And then... with an interruption in my sleep, I would sit up in the middle of the night thinking that the chest came over and nudged me to wake up. Funny how your mind plays tricks on you when you are obsessed with something, and only seven years old. Oh how I wished that I could be like Little Tom and not be bothered by such a dumb thing as that darn chest.

During the day I had plenty to do and other things to think about to keep my mind off of the trunk. I was making a whip and learning how to tan skins. Once or twice when we were just sitting around talking, I would almost ask Gramps what was in the chest, but I could not get up the courage to ask him what was in it.

I even went as far to sleep outside one night, to be away from the compulsion to look in the trunk that haunted me. Telling Gramps that it was too hot inside the shack that night to sleep. I didn't do that again because it was too uncomfortable sleeping on the ground and it actually was hotter outside with all the bugs and such than it was inside.

Once, when Gramps was in the cabin, I stood in the doorway and watched him to see if he went to the chest to open it, but no-such-luck. He just dug through the pelts and picked out the ones he wanted to take and sell the next time we went to town. But never once did he even go near the irritating object of my obsession.

Maybe I could pretend that Little Tom was missing. And when we were looking for him, we would just happen to have to look into the trunk to see if he was in there, but I knew that story sounded dumb because how would Little Tom get in there in the first place. Well scrub that idea.

Another idea was, the next time Gramps wanted to go to town, I would stay here and wait until he was out of sight and then get my peek inside that cantankerous old chest. Nah, I couldn't do that to Gramps. Not after all he has done for me. Gramps was more like kin to me than just a good friend and protector. No... I couldn't sneak behind his back no more than I could have done that to my own father.

So I guess for now I will just have to hold back my insatiable interest to see what was inside the dirty old chest.

Chapter 18

The days turned into weeks and I became very happy.

My first whip was finished and we were going to town to sell skins, pelts and possibly the whip that I made. Gramps said it was a fine piece of workmanship.

"What kind of mark are ya gona put on yore whip?" he said while checking out the quality of the whip.

"Mark?... What kind of mark do you mean?" I replied.

"Well ya see when ya makes a real quality item such as dis whip, ya wants to put some kind of a mark on it. Yore own mark. Kind of like a brand, to let people know who made dis fine whip," he went on.

"Kind of like a trade mark that would stay with da item forever. Dis would let people know that yore whips are the best they is."

"But what should I put on it and where?"

"Well dats up to ya, but whatever ya puts on it gots to be the same every time. It would be yurs and nobody else's. I would put da mark on the handle to the top by da deer hide," he explained to me.

"Yes sir, that would be where I'd put it, if'n I was to do it caus it would have less ware thar."

He went on to say, "Ya needs to thin bout it fer a bit so ya comes up wit a real gooden."

I thought about it for a considerable long time and finely I had it. I was going to carve a small bird in the handle with my initials beside it. Like the bird that I showed Pa that I did in school.

The next day we went to the town called Rattlesnake Pass and Gramps went to take care of his business at the place where he sold the skins. I waited outside and played with my whip. I wasn't too strong so I couldn't make it crack very good but I still thought it sounded pretty fair. I thought that as I grew bigger I would be able to make a much better sound with a whip.

"Boy what ya got thar?" said a big burly man that was tying his cowpony up at the hitching post. The man was obviously a cowman with a very interesting long handlebar mustache underneath a generous hooked-beak nose.

I was some what startled by the big man and didn't know what to think when he spoke to me.

"It's a cracker whip that I made, sir."

The man wore worn faded blue-jeans under his shoddy looking chafes. A blue and white plaid shirt was tucked into his jeans with a large red scarf around his neck. He also wore a very sizeable gray hat pulled forward on his head covering his long brown shaggy hair. Like Gramps, the cowman wore a revolver in a holster on his belt only unlike Gramps, his revolver was in the front. Also, he had a very used working knife on the belt tucked into the back. The revolver is what I noticed the most because where I stood in front of the man, that is what I saw the most.

"Naaa ya-all didn't make it, did ya?"

"Yes sir, I did. My grandpa showed me how to make it and he said it turned out to be a very fine whip."

I could see the cow man was very interested in it and I said, " Do you want to take a better look at it, maybe try it out?"

"Ya I sure would," he said as I handed it to him.

He took a few steps forward so that his pony and me would be out of the way and began to work with it.

BANG, BANG, BANG was the sound the whip made.

"A heeeeee-e-e-e ah," the drover let out a high pitched scream as he worked the whip.

BANG... it went again. The noise sounded like Mr. Sands forty caliber gun going off.

"Ya-hooo."

I couldn't believe my ears as to how loud the cow-man made the whip sound.

"A heeeeee-e-e-e ah," he yelled again raising the cow whip over his head and bringing it back with the loud whack.

I don't know if it was my imagination or what but I even thought I saw a small whiff of smoke come off the end of the whip when it went BANG.

Out came Gramps and the proprietor from the building where Gramps was doing his dealings to see what the noise was all about.

"What's going on out cheer?" the store owner said seeing the big man with Timmy. "What ya doing wit that boy?"

"Ya the boy's Grandpa?" the man said looking at the silver-haired man without the apron.

Gramps eyed the man from top to bottom and said, "Yep... I surly am."

"What's da boy did?" he asked.

BANG, went the whip again. BANG, BANG.

"The boy ain't done nothin but he tells me that he made this cheer really fine whip."

"The boy did make da whip, why did ya want to know?"

"Caus I'm in the need of a real good cow whip like dis un," he said.

BANG went the whip again. BANG, BANG. "Woow -e-e-e-e, Woow-e-e-e-e" he said.

"Do ya think the boy would sell dis un to me?"

"I don't know, why don't ya ask him if'n he would part with such a fine whip as dat?" Gramps said.

I just stood there looking at the two men talking and wondering what was going to happen next.

"Boy, what is yore given name?"

"Sir, my name is Timmy."

"Well Mr. Timmy, would ya be a-willen to part with

dis cheer whip?" the cowman said, not able to stop working the whip.

"Now don't git me wrong, I be willin to pay ya a very good amount fer it."

After watching Gramps dicker with the skins, I knew that he always started the dickering by asking what the person buying wanted to pay for them. That way he got some idea of what he had in mind to pay and what he was going to ask for them.

"Well I did have a massive amount of time in making the whip and it even has my brand on it, but, I guess I would be willing to sell it for a price." I said.

"What did you have in mind in paying for this fine whip?" I went on, edging the cow man to come up with a price and hoping it would be high.

"Go ahead and make it crack again to see how good the sound is and look at the quality of the handle and the beautiful deer skin that I used on the whip." This was what Gramps would do with his skins... show the good qualities of the product that you are selling so that's all they could think about.

BANG, off it went again.

"Yes dis is a very fine whip. Probably one of da best

that I ever seen, and I can see ya gots a powerful lot of time in making it. I can offer ya ten fer it." he said still looking at the smooth finish of the handle and getting the feel of it.

Thinking that all he wanted to pay was ten cents for the whip I frowned and said, "For all the work and the high quality material that I used?"

Gramps sat down on a crate and laughed to himself, knowing that the man meant ten dollars and that was a very good price for it in these times. And that if I could get that much money for it I would be very happy.

BANG! It went again. The impressed cow man continued working the whip.

"Well boy, I really likes da whip so I am willen to go to twelve fer it."

Again I thought twelve cents, I knew that it was my first one but I did think it was worth more then twelve cents for it.

I said as I reached for the whip, "No, I think it's worth a heap more than that."

I was hoping that I could get at least a silver dollar for it and after all this was the first cow man that looked at it, so I was going to take my time and see if I could get a silver dollar for it from somebody else.

Reluctant to let go of the whip the man said, "Boy... ya really knows how to drive up a mean bargain. Ya got me at a good time fer ya, cause I gest got paid and I kin offer ya fifteen silver dollars fer da whip. Now dats my very best offer, I caint go any higher fer it cus I wuz a countin on getin it fer a lot less."

My mouth opened wide and I couldn't believe my ears when the cow man said, fifteen silver dollars. FIFTEEN SILVER DOLLARS!

BANG, BANG, BANG.

"Okay you just bought yourself a fine whip, and you said I drove a hard bargain."

The man counted out fifteen shinny silver dollars and as he did he asked me if I could make a couple more whips because he knew two friends that were looking for somebody to make them high quality cow whips.

"Yes sir I can, but it will take a couple of weeks before I can have them. But will you do one thing for me?" I asked him.

"Sure Mr. Timmy what kin I do fer ya?"

"Please don't tell your friends how much you paid because you got such a good price and that the next one will have to cost more."

Gramps came over and told the cow man what a good deal he got and had to remind him of course he was taking advantage of a youngen.

"Ya can count on me young feller, an ya kin charge dem boys what ever ya want cause they makes more money than I do. And I will tell em they has to buy the only ones with yur brand on em." then he bid me a good farewell.

The cowman looked about his pony to make sure his rolled-up poncho, slicker and cotton blanket were snuggly secured before he mounted, and then rode slowly out of town, occasionally cracking the whip to see how his horse took to the noise. BANG! BANG! "A heeeeee-e-e-e ah."

We could hear the whip crack at least a good thirty minutes down the road even after the cow man was out of sight.

Chapter 19

Gramps explained that the fifteen silver dollars was a great deal of money and that I should think about saving part of my money for a rainy day. I didn't understand what that meant because it rained here almost every day.

I was surprised that he said that all the money was for me. I tried to share the money with Gramps but he refused saying, "Ya made da whip all by yore self and the skins dat ya used didn't add up to nothin. Ya deserve what ya made fer it, even if it was a lot more than I would think ya would git."

I asked Gramps if it would be alright if I bought Jull something for teaching me the fine art of making whips and he said that would be a very charitable gesture.

"What do you recommend, not knowing

what to buy an Indian woman." I asked.

"Well see an Injun woman ain't like a normal woman. They don't likes or use fancy things like a white women. But she did tell me if'n I could see my way to buy her a new skinning knife dat she would like it beins her old un is plum worn out."

"Well that is what I will get her. Will you help me pick out a good one for her?"

While we were at the dry-goods store picking out a skinning knife for Jull I saw some small cans of paint on the shelf. I asked how much they were and the man said that he would let me have all seven cans for one dollar, but couldn't understand why I would want them. I also asked if he had any small brushes.

"We don't git much request fer paint not alone brushes, but I do have two one inch brushes somewhere around here and I will just give them to ya if'n I kin find them. Ah-ha here they are. After all what am I gona do wit brushes without paint?" he said looking for a box to put the paint cans in.

Gramps didn't understand what I wanted the paint for either but said it was my money and I could spend it on what ever I wanted.

We did find a right nice skinning knife that I talked him into selling it for another silver dollar. But guess what, I got him to include a bag of stripped hard candy in the deal.

"Yore just as bad as yore Gramps and now I got two of ya fellers to deal wit."

The store owner said as he bagged up my order, "I'll try to be prepared for ya boys da next time ya comes to town."

Grandpa Sands finished dickering on his order and we left to go get our root beer and a cold beer for the old man. Then on our way back to the cabin a man stopped us on the road going out of town.

"Sir I couldn't help hear that the boy called you Grandpa in the trading store, can I ask your name and where is the boy's parents?"

"Well it ain't none of yore business." He said looking right in the mans face.

"I'm sorry, sir, my name is Clyde Strum and I am in charge of the county orphanage over in Collier county. Here are my credentials."

As the man displayed an official looking document to gramps he said, "You see we are looking for a boy about this boys age that ran away from the town of Buzzard Bay a couple of weeks ago. I don't mean to be rude but the boy we are looking for just lost both of his parents and we are very concerned about the boy."

"That don't gives ya the right to just stop any boy ya sees on da road," Gramps said in an annoying tone of voice.

"Caint ya see dis boy is fine and healthy, not at all like somebody dat had run away like ya said."

"I do beg your forgiveness' for the bother but the boy fits the description of the boy that is missing, and I am just checking all children of that description."

"Well dis boy is my grandson and I don't has to prove anything to ya," Gramps said with his hand on the handle of his revolver.

The man apologized again for disturbing us, turned away, and got on his horse and went back to town.

"Boy ya kin stop tremblen now, that man and no other man is gonna take ya away from me. Ya is my grandson if I say so no matter what anybody says."

I felt great comfort in the words the old man said, if only it was true and he was really my true Grand Pa.

Once we got back to the cabin I gave Jull the skinning knife that we selected for her and she was grateful for it in her own elusive way by just nodding her head, twisting her mouth in a smile and saying, "Uhh." I guess a smile is the same in any language.

I was surprised to see that I got several different colors of paint and I asked Gramps if I could do some painting inside of the cabin.

"Thar ain't nothin in that old shack worth wasting paint on, but if ya wants to use yore paint on anything in thar... ya kin," he said, patting me on the head.

"Thanks Gramps, I will do a good job and make you proud of me," I said anxious to get started on my very first art undertaking.

I first fixed in my mind the beautiful blue swamp and the wide variety of birds and trees that I could envision. Then I looked around to see what was available to paint on and fixed my eyes on the two unmatched

chairs with their flat boards on the seats. Yes, that would be a good place to start. I remembered that Pa always started with a background and then he would put in the most important part of the painting. I nervously pried opened all seven cans of paint and commenced to create the background on the chairs. While one seat was drying I painted the background on the other and then went to work on painting birds nesting in the trees on the dryer chair. Then I repeated a similar scene on the other chair including the flat board of the back of this one.

Gramps being very curious as to what I was doing started to look into the cabin and I said, "Don't come in yet, I'll tell you when I am finished and then you can come in."

The old man said to the Indian, "I don't know what that boy is up to but he seems to be happy, and that makes me happy."

I was all fired up after the chairs and more at ease now and ready to start something larger. My eyes were plastered to the top of the aged wobbly table. I thought of the beautiful breathtaking sunsets that we enjoyed at the shack where I lived. I must have had an artistic explosion as I picked up a loaded paint brush full of bright red paint and smashed it into the table top. Then taking up the brush with a large glob of blue paint and smashing it hard onto the table. Again and again went the brush loaded with paint. I was having so much fun at times I would let out little squeak sounds like, "Yea, Oh yea, or Yep I like that."

Mr. Sands heard me and wondered if there was anything wrong.

"Are ya okay in thar boy?"

"Yes sir, just fine... just fine."

At times the masterpiece took on the view of the side of a gaudy grotesque circus wagon.

I worked feverously and when I was finished... I stepped back and looked at what I created. I had to lean back against the cot with amazement at what I saw. I couldn't believe that I was the one to put paint to this artwork. I thought to myself that if my father was looking down on me, he would be very proud of what I just did. I sat on the cot for a few minutes to get my composure and asked Little Tom what he thought but all he did was purr and that was good enough for me.

It turned out to be the most brilliant sunset ever painted and I thought for sure that my Pa helped move my hand when I was painting it.

My mind raced with ideas. "What can I do to top the painting that I just did?" I thought to myself.

It had to be something that would be the grand conclusion of what I was doing. Something that people would be talking about for years... if the outside world would be able to see it. Pictures of different birds pop into my head, no I already did that on the chairs. Maybe I could paint a painting of the town of Buzzard Bay. No, I don't want to do that, too many fresh bad memories. Than it finally came to me what I wanted to paint but I needed something large to paint on. The old rustic chest that I was so drawn to, no, not big enough. Beside I might be too tempted to look inside. As I scratched my head and looked at the wall by the cot I saw the perfect place to put my masterpiece. I could see in my mind's

eye the only painting that would work on the wall and I immediately got to work.

I worked for what I thought was hours and it was getting late and the sun would be going down in another hour. Beside I was running out of paint so I wouldn't be able to paint much more anyway.

Finished, I thought that I was finally finished and I put my brush down. The last bright light of the setting sun came rushing through the door and abruptly landed on the bright scenery that I just painted across the wall.

"Okay you can come in now, but be careful... the paint may still be wet on some things," I said putting the lids back on the paint cans.

"Timmy!" Gramps said with his mouth wide open.

He stood in the doorway and just stared inside the room. I didn't know if this was a good sign or not. I wasn't sure if I went too far and painted more that what I

should have done.

Eventually he gained his composure and said, "Lord above... my eyes have died and went to God's land."

He took his hat off in a kind of reverent motion and then ran his fingers through his silver hair. "Boy ya must be touched by an angel, I can't tell the wall from the outside. It looks just like I'm outside in the big blue swamp."

What I painted was a swamp scene with Grandpa Sands as he looked when we were in the swamp and he shot the gator on the first hunt we went on.

"Ahhh," is the sound that came from the Indian, and believe me that was a lot for her.

"Boy you have a real talent, these pictures look so real that the birds can almost fly away," the old man exclaimed in great surprise at what he saw.

I sat back on the cot just bursting with boyish pride.

"Thank you, I did this because it was the only way I could possibly repay you for all you have done for me."

Gramps came over and gave me a great big hug and said, "This calls fer a celebration with some striped hard candy."

I made my bed outside that night because the smell of

the paint was too strong, but it sure was a lot of fun doing all of the painting. I knew that I was hooked and thought that the next time I was going to try to do something even more impressive and maybe someday, well who knows.

Chapter 20

The paint dried to a beautiful sheen in a couple of days. The wall painting took on life of it's own and Gramps was right, it looked like it was right outside.

I started doing chores around the cabin and it made me feel more like I was part of a family again. Although it was a strange kind of family, a seven year old run-away orphan boy, a wild old swamp man and a silent Seminole Indian woman. Oh yes I almost forgot a couple of squirrels and a wily little old black tom cat.

I began work on two more whips. Two, because Gramps said that I can make two at a time just as easy as one.

"Why don't I work on five or ten at a time?" I asked thinking that it would make them better and faster if they were in larger quantity.

Gramps shaking his head while rubbing his two week old beard said, "No, if ya would do too many at a time the work on dem would start to be shoddy and ya would have a hard time sellin dem."

Handing me strips of deer hide to braid he went on, "See if'n ya only work on no more den two at a time, ya kin take yore time and do a better job. That way da quality will be good and dem cow men will want to buy um."

I caught Gramps going into the cabin a lot more often since I did the paintings. He didn't go in to do anything, but he just stood looking at the paintings and mumbling to himself.

"Timmy has ya got dem whips finished up yet?"

I handed the one that was finished to him and said, "I should have the other one finished by this evening."

He took a good long look at the one I handed him and then began working it. BANG! BANG, BANG was the loud sound that came as the old man skillfully worked the whip. The sound echoed through the trees jolting the birds off their branches making them fly. Even the Indian woman came around the cabin to see what the noise was.

"Boy ya done real good on dis un. I would think dis

un will go fast and for even more money den ya got fer da first un," he said with a big smile on his face.

"If ya git da other un done tonight we kin go to town tomorrow. Jull needs more supplies," he said. "And I bet ya will sell dem whips fast."

I felt like I was truly fitting in with Gramps, even though I wasn't his for real grandson. But he made me feel like I was. Even asking me of my opinion of what skins I thought he should take to town to sell.

After Mr. Sands sold his skins we went to the trading goods store and since I didn't see any cow men in the street, I went inside with Gramps.

"Howdy boys, I thought it was bout time ya-all was coming to town. I just got some new skinning knifes in if'n ya-all was needin any?"

"Nope, we just needs supplies dis time," said Gramps.

The store owner noticed that I was holding the two whips that I brought to town and said, "Hey boy is that one of the famous whips that ya makes?"

"I don't know about famous but I did make these cow whips, sir," I said.

"I brought them to sell to the cow men but I didn't

see any in town."

Gramps went about gathering the supplies that we needed and just let the store owner talk to me.

"Oh them boys are down to the saloon. They been here bout an hour and I speck they are just bout ready to go back to the ranch. Kin I take a look at one of them whips, sonny boy?"

I handed one to him and said, "Yes sir, here you are."

He stepped outside and made a loud crack with it and then tried it again.

Coming back inside he said, "Boy ya got some fine whip thar. I will buy the two ya-all brought wit ya today and then I will buy all ya bring the next time, if'n that would be okay with your grandpa?"

Gramps let out his loud bull frog laugh and said, "Ya don't have to ask me, them whips belong to da boy. And he is his own man."

"Boy, I will give ya eight shinny silver dollars fer each one of them whips ya sell me."

"No sir, I got more than that for the first one I sold."

"Well I kin go up to nine dollars but not a cent more. After all I got to make a liven off what I buy, so I would have to make a profit on what I sell. And I would be buying all that you make, ya wouldn't have to do any work selling them."

Just then something in my memory told me to say no to the proposal that was made. I remembered what my Pa said, "If you got a talent to do something and you kin sell what you make, try to sell it yourself and keep all of the money. Why should you give a part of the money with anybody?"

"No sir, I think I will sell my whips to the cow men myself," I said with confidence.

The storeowner looked at Gramps with a look of question and Gramps just shrugged his shoulders.

"The boy knows what he's doin, and ya knows he right not to sell dem to ya," Gramps said.

The store owner wasn't upset that he couldn't buy the whips and said, "Well ya caint blame me for not tryin. Here let's still be friends and have a piece of hard candy on the house."

The old man came over to where they were and said, "How bout me, after all I'm da boy's Grandpa?"

Looking at Gramps sorrowful look the proprietor said, "That don't qualify ya fer a free piece of candy but I feels sorry fer ya. Ya old fart."

"Oh by da way, thar was a feller said he was from Collier county orphanage home in cheer after ya was cheer da last time. He was askin bout little Timmy. If'n I knew where he came from, and if'n Timmy is yore real grandson. I told him that it weren't none of my business but as fer as I was concerned that Timmy was yore own boy."

I reached out for Mr. Sands hand.

"He said that he would be back to question ya again and if ya didn't cooperate, he would bring the sheriff wit him."

"He did, did he? Well Timmy's my grandson and ain't nobody gonna take the boy from me," he said.

We finished our business at the trading store and went to the saloon so Gramps could get his beer and I could get a root beer. On the way there he said, "Ya don't have to worry bout that county man takin ya from me because that just ain't gonna happen."

We got our drinks and I sold both whips for sixteen dollars each. The cow men were happy and said that they knew at least two more men that might buy a whip the next time I came to town. I gave the money to Gramps to hold for me and I felt a little better after I sold the whips but I still had concerns in the back of my mind that my life with him might all end.

Chapter 21

Clyde Strum, setting patiently in the blistering hot sun was waiting about two miles down the dirt road from town.

We only had about a half mile before the turn off that took us back through the swamp to the cabin. This time the man was paired up with another man that turned out to be the sheriff of this Monroe County.

Gramps said, “stay close to me and do just what I tell ya to do,” and we moved closer to the two men.

“Mr. Sands... This is the sheriff Wilbur Rudd of Monroe County. He’s just with me so that we don’t have any trouble when I question you about this boy that you claim is your grandson,” the man said in a tone of timid unsure authority.

“I don‘t have to answer any of yore boring questions," Gramps said standing his ground.

"Calm down Mr. Sands, all you have to do is answer a couple of Mr. Strums questions and if you can prove that you are the boys real relative, we will leave you alone," said the good looking young sheriff dismounting his horse. He wasn't a full sheriff, he explained, just a deputy that was sent out on inconsequential matters.

"Were not here to harm anybody, just give the boy, if he is the one that we are looking for, the best of care."

"Yes sir... ya-all want to take him to the Collier County Orphanage Home and put him to work in the cane fields. That's what ya-all wants to do, I ain't no dummy. Besides Timmy ain't no run-away, he's my grandson and that's all I am gonna say about the matter. Now git outa my way, my stomach is starting to growl."

I saw that the man that I called Gramps was really getting mad and I was afraid that he was about to do something very bad because he had his hand on the handle of his revolver. I started to sob. I didn't want Gramps to do anything that would get him in a lot of trouble. I didn't want to go back to Collier with those men but I didn't want anything to happen to my friend and protector either.

“Gramps...” I pleaded.

“Timmy, yas okay and thar ain’t nothin to be worried bout. Ya are my boy and some how I will prove it to these fellers,” he said in a calming voice.

“Well Mr. Sands how are you going prove that this boy is who you say he is,” said Mr. Strum. “Do you have any proof of who Timmy is or who is his parents are and where they are right now?”

I know that Mr. Sands could not prove who I was and I knew if he could tell them that my parents were dead and buried in a little cemetery in Collier county that I would be making a trip back to a place that I didn’t want to go. It seems it would be up to me to stop Gramps from doing something very, very bad. But I knew that the old man that I so warmly called Gramps could not tell them where my parents were and who I really was.

I said, “Sir...” and Gramps stopped me by putting his hand to my mouth and pulling me to stand in back of him.

Gramps spoke in a toned down voice now, “Boys lets all go to my cabin and we could have a little touch of shine and maybe I can clear up this whole problem. Tie up yore horses cheer cause it‘s too hard going for horses."

The men hesitantly agreed to go to the cabin but I was still apprehensive. Very worried that when Gramps got the two men back in the swamp and after the gators and other wild life got done with their bodies, nobody would be able to find them. It was my opinion that this man that I looked up to was a peaceful man in all respects of the word, but I also thought he would fight with all he had to protect what he believed in. Mr. Sands was a pretty wild person and if pushed... he might push back pretty hard. I thought to myself, *"Oh Lord, please don't let anything happen to these men and especially don't let anything happen to Gramps."*

About half way to the cabin one of the men stopped at the edge of the water, wet a scarf, and wiped his head and said, "How far is this cabin of yours? This sun is about to cook my brains out and my throat is getting mighty parched."

Gramps was taking a new way to the cabin that I never saw before and it was pretty rough walking. This route to the cabin was about twice as long and made me more uneasy about what was going to happen. Again to myself I said a prayer that nothing would happen to anyone.

"Oh it's just a short ways down here now," Mr. Sands said. "Just beyond dis small swamp."

"I hate to complain but this proof that you are going to show us better be worth it," said Clyde Strum pushing away a mulberry bush.

"That's for sure," said the young sheriff deputy kicking some mud off his boots. "I just got these new boots and I don't like breaking them in this way."

Gramps stopped and replied roughly, "Oh stop yore complaining, ya wanted proof and I am gonna show ya proof."

Just then I saw the clearing in the swamp with the cabin. I could not understand why the old man brought us this way but he must have had his reason. *"God we are here, now what should I do?"*

Gramps said, "Ya boys should be honored because ain't nobody ever been back cheer and I wants to keep it that way. Come on boys let's us go into da cabin to git out of dis sun."

I stood back and watched Gramps standing in the doorway of the cabin still rubbing a smooth spot on the handle of his revolver. I caught his eyes and pleaded with my eyes not to do anything.

"Wow what beautiful paintings! Who is the artist?" said the sheriff.

"Yes these are really pretty pictures, I understand the boy that we are looking for is very good at this kind of work," said Clyde Strum.

Just then Little Tom jumped off the cot where he was sleeping, and the sheriff picked him up and commented what a cute little cat he was.

"Yes he is pretty cute," said Mr. Strum. "I think this Timmy Dalton that we are looking for has a little black cat too."

"Gramps...! I said.

Timmy, everythin is okay. Why don't you go down a ways an check da possum traps?"

I turned toward the swamp and ran as fast as I could. Jumping over the fence with skins stretched on it I tripped and fell to the ground. Mr. Strum came to the door of the cabin and said, "Where is the boy going?"

I jumped up and continued to run toward the swamp.

Gramps put his hand on the mans shoulder and with his revolver in his other hand said, "Oh da boy's just gonna check on da traps. He'll be right back soon. Did ya say the boy that ya is lookin fer is named Timmy Dalton?"

The sheriff was unarmed and said, "Hey, what you planning on doing with that fire arm, old man?"

Gramps pushed Clyde Strum back in the cabin and said, "I don't plan on doin notten with it I just wanted to git yore tention. I asked ya did ya say the boy yore lookin fer is named Timmy Dalton?"

"Yes... that's the boys name, Timothy Dalton. Now put away that revolver so we can talk this over like reasonable men," Strum said.

The old man grabbed his hat, brandished it above him and burst into laughter all the while jumping around in a down-homey type of a jig. He stamped so hard in the dirt floor that small dust clouds formed, making Mr. Strum wave his arms to clear the air.

"My God man, what is wrong with you?" said Wilbur Rudd.

Gramps put his revolver back in his holster and said, "Sorry bout that... I just got so excited about what I am gonna show ya." Still laughing in his bull-frog laugh he said, "Come on and sit down on the boy's bird paintings and I will git out da shine so we kin relax."

Gramps even pulled the chairs out for the men to sit on and then got out a jug of moon shine and found three clean cups to pour the shine in. By then I think I must have been to the edge of the Big Blue Cypress Swamp where I stopped to catch my breath. I was happy that so far I didn't hear the terrible echo sound from the revolver that Gramps held on the two men. I did not know if the two men overpowered the old man and took his fire arm away from him and I had a vision that they tied him up and now they were hot on the trail looking for me. I knew that I had a head start and I did have an advantage over them because I knew the swamp... somewhat. I was so terribly sorry that I got Mr. Sands into all this trouble because he was so kind to me and treated me just like I was his very own grandson without even knowing what my last name was or who my parents were.

"Yes sir, yes sir, ya boys ain't gonna believe what I'm gonna show ya," Mr. Sands said still thrashing around.

"Okay now that we had a drink, let's get back to why we are really here," said Mr. Clyde Strum.

"Ya sure ya don't want another hit on the jug," Gramps said with a curious smile on his face.

It was quite warm in the cabin and the two men were getting impatient and just wanted to get it over with.

The sheriff stood up and looked out the door to see if he could see Timmy and said, "Come on old man, quit trying to delay. Show us some proof that you are the boy's real grandpa or we will have to go look for the boy. It's getting late and I can see some pretty dark clouds a brewing and I don't want to get caught in a storm. It's bad enough that I got mud all over my new boots."

The old man started moving pelts off the chest and said with a chuckle, "Ya really did say that the boys family name is Dalton? That would be Timothy Dalton... is that right? Dalton...! Dalton! I can't possibly believe it my self."

"Yes, yes, now come on quite stalling around and show us what we came here for," said the sheriff. He talked with a little strength in his voice thinking that if the old man were going to do something to hurt them, he would have done it by now.

"Now let me see, where did I put dat?" The swamp man said with a big grin on his face as he poked around the old dilapidated chest, pulling out some old garments at first and finally hoisting out a small metal box that was wrapped in a beaver skin. He untied the pelt and found the lid was rusted shut. He pulled out his hunting knife and worked on the lid until it popped open.

As he rummaged through the box he found what he was looking for, "Yes... dare it is," and he pulled out an aged wrinkled photo. On the photo was an image of a young couple at a church getting married. He wiped off a small bit of grime from the photo and handed it to Mr. Strum.

"Well I see a nice young couple that looks like they are getting married at a pleasant little church, what does that have to do with Timmy Dalton?" he said looking at the photo in the light coming through the door way.

"Turn it over, turn it over," Gramps said so excited with laughter that he was almost crying. "That is a photo of my daughter when she got married to Hector Dalton! And... Hector Dalton is da boy's Pa."

The stunned man turned the photo over and on the back of the photo in indigo blue ink was written; Grace Sands, daughter of Marion and Jules Sands is married to Hector Dalton on July 23, 1922.

Mr. Sands acted as shocked as the man from the orphanage was and said, "Da Lord has really blessed me on dis day, amen."

"Well I'll be a monkey's uncle, that makes ya Timmy's real Grandpa," said the sheriff standing up. "Well that's good enough fer me, I guess our business cheer is done."

Mr. Strum apologized to Marion Sands, bringing him up to date he told him what happened to Timmy's parents and that he was sorry about the loss of his daughter. He also told him where they were buried if he wanted to take Timmy back to visit them some day. "Mr. Sands, again I am sorry for bothering you and I assure you that we won't be of any bother to you again. I am just glad that Timmy is safe and in your very good hands." He handed the photo back to Gramps and said, "You best keep this in a good place so it doesn't get lost. I am sure the good people of Buzzard Bay will be happy to hear that the boy is safe and healthy. You do need to see about getting the boy into school sometime."

Gramps shook the hands of the two men and said that he would take them back out to the road if they promised not to tell anybody where he lived. They made such a statement and off they went.

“Don’t you think we should all go look for Timmy? It‘s starten to look purty bad out south, I kin hear the roar a‘ comin,” said the sheriff.

“It does look like we are going to get a good down pour,” said Mr. Strum.

“Naw, da boy knows da swamp almost as good as me and he probably will be back cheer by da time I gits back.”

Chapter 22

I went farther into the swamp than I had ever been with Mr. Sands. I was so afraid of what must have happened at the cabin and I still thought that the two mean men were after me. A thought came to me, about what the old man tried to tell me that I shouldn't blame God for my misgivings but it was very hard for me not to blame Him. After all what did I do to deserve all of the bad things that have happened to me, and who knows what is going to happen to me if and when they catch up with me. I must keep going... there was no way that Mr. Strum and the sheriff were going to catch me and take me to an orphanage home. I wished that I could have brought Little Tom but I knew he would be safe with the man I was allowed to call Gramps. At least Little Tom would not have to go to an orphanage and I knew the old man would take care of him no matter what was going to happen to me.

I moved into a clearing to try to judge what time it was but curious dark clouds had developed and were covering up the sun. Long rumbling sounds were off in the distance making me believe that it was just heat thunder, a sound that was quite common this time of the year in Florida.

After catching my breath and taking notice of the surrounding area that I was in I decided to find the Seminole Indian village that Ghost Swamp Flower lived when she wasn't helping Mr. Sands. Maybe if I could find it, I could hide there with the old Indian woman. The trouble was I didn't know what direction the village was.

There was that thundering sound again as a gust of wind blew a large clump of Spanish moss from a enormous dead cypress tree on top of my head pushing my hat forward over my eyes. Before I could adjust my hat from my face I stumbled face first into the green murky water next to a group of cypress knees. Reaching for a stump to pull myself up I was jolted to my senses by a four foot alligator with his huge mouth open just a couple of feet away from where I fell. I fumbled for my knife and before I could get it out to challenge the beast, he vanished under the dark murky water.

I seized the moment and pulled myself out of the water and laid on the wet sandy soil trembling. Another blast of air blew a cold chill over me. I remembered about a half hour must have passed and I thought that I better get going again, considering Mr. Strum had a good chance to catch up with me by now. But which way should I go? At this time I was lost and was wondering to myself if I wouldn't be better off going back and giving myself up. But I was all twisted around and I didn't know where back was.

A fast moving shower pelted me and added to the misery that I felt. The sky grew darker and the air was

filled with static electricity. I wished this late summer storm was over but the farther I went the harder the rain came. Wild wind outbursts that were strong enough to bend small trees and bringing down large branches from large cypress trees pushed me from side to side. Birds and small animals were acting strange, dashing from one place or another. This didn't seem like a typical summer storm. Flashes of light so bright that for a split second looked like it was daylight came from the lightning. I huddled at the base of a hollowed out cypress tree to get shelter.

By now the sky was totally black except for the constant flashes of white spider webs from the lightning.

I was terrified, more afraid then I have ever been. I was even more afraid now then when my parents didn't come home. At least at that time I had hope that they were coming back. But now I had no hope. No hope of my parents coming to save me. No hope of being able to stay with Mr. Sands all though he said he was my grandpa. And now, I didn't know where I was. Even if Mr. Strum and the sheriff could find me, and right now I almost wished that they would, all I had to look forward to was living in an orphanage home with strangers for the rest of my life.

I didn't think that Gramps was really my grandpa and if he was able to some how come up with some wild story to make Mr. Strum think that he was my grandpa they surely would check into it later and then take me away anyway. So I would be back right where I started from. *Why has God brought on so much torment to me.*

A brilliant flash of electricity struck the tree that I was taking sanctuary under and forced me to the ground. It was like God was trying to send me a message. *Get up Timmy, get up and go find Gramps.* I got up and ran.

I don't know how many times I fell and then tried to get up to run farther into the swamp. I could feel the charge in the air and the sound of the wind was deafening and the oxygen that I tried to breath was being sucked from my body. The lightning made war on me as I ran from one tree to another. Small fires started around me putting pine trees and cypress alike to blaze, without the success of the pelting rain to put out the fires.

I remembered that either I stumbled trying to escape a nearby fire or I was knocked out by a bolt of lightning. I don't know, and I can't say how long I was unconscious, but when I awoke I was being tied to the base of a very large palm tree. When my eyes started to focus, I could see what I thought was a large white figure that was tying me to the tree. No it wasn't a white person, it was the albino black man, Mos.

"Is yus okay, boy?" Mos said shouting over the noise of the storm.

"Uhh... I think so, but what are you doing to me?" I didn't do anything to him but I thought he caught me and was tying me up to keep me here for the sheriff.

The albino tried to comfort me and said, "Yus gona has to stay here till the storm is over, I don't has time to git yus to safety. Thars a bigen comin, but yus be safe cheer. Just hold on wit all yus might and pray. Pray boy, like yus never did bfor."

As he started to run off a tall cypress tree was pulled up by it's roots and only missed Mos by inches and he yelled back at me, "The old Indian woman and Mr. Sands is out looking fer yus and they sent me to look for yus too."

"Mos," I screamed.

"Don't leave me! Please don't leave me!" I continued to scream.

The wind was so loud that I barely heard him as I

struggled to free myself, “Why did you tie me to this tree?” I yelled to him.

He did say that the old Indian woman and Mr. Sands were looking for me and that must mean that Gramps was able to get loose from his ropes that bound him and was okay.

The rain ran down my face and mingled with my tears making it hard to see the albino’s figure running off in distance. I was able to make out from what he was saying that I should stay tied to the palm tree through the storm and I would be safe. Right after that the wind picked up with a tremendous force and I thought I could see Mos being picked up and blown away.

The palm tree shook and vibrated so hard I felt I would slide out of the rope that held me. I could feel it move and bend half way over, but it did not fall over.

“Mos...!” I screamed with no answer to my cries.

Flashes of light were all around me but I still could not see Mos. I just tried to hold onto the palm tree and prayed that the lightning would not strike it. I prayed... I prayed hard. I prayed that the fires wouldn’t get me. I prayed that Gramps and the old Indian woman were okay. I prayed that the albino black man that was trying to save me, was safe. And I prayed that this terrible storm would be over soon.

I pressed my face hard into the palm to try to keep the flying twigs from hitting me so hard in the face. I fell in and out of awareness. My arms felt like they were about to pull out of my shoulders and my legs hung like dead anchor weights. Whenever there was no lightning flashes, it would become completely black except for the fires off in the distance.

"Mos...! Gramps...! Is there anybody out there?" I was screaming as loud as my lungs could produce sound.

How could all this be happening to me? I am only seven years old, but I don't know if I am going to make it to eight the way my life is going.

Chapter 23

For an instant the air grew calm and the unrelenting lightning let up. The appearance of the sky turned lighter and I could see fast moving gray clouds with patches of blue flashing through them. This reprieve was short lived. Catching my breath, I thought the storm was finally over but as I started to try to untie the ropes that held me to the palm tree, the wind and rain picked up again. Expecting the worst, I braced myself and buried my face into the tree and shielded my head with my arms.

****

Mr. Sands made it back to the shack after taking Mr. Strum and Sheriff Rudd up to the road just as the hurricane began. Pulling skins off the fence he was driven to the ground by a powerful squall of air. Just as he got to his feet, he was hit by a tree branch producing a heavy cut to his forehead.

In a daze he staggered inside the cabin and wiped clean the wound then wrapped a bandage on his head and made sure the frightened cat was safe, then left to look for Timmy.

The old man tried to call out to Timmy but the sound from his voice was muffled over by the noise the wind made. Flying debris whizzed by him and made the going almost impossible to continue. He thought he knew where he was but the landscape had already started to change. Cypress trees were toppled over and there was new water holes where they weren't before. Large mounds of debris was forming as the wind blew the smaller trees and brush together making it even more confusing. Along with Gramps, animals with a great fear of the storm, were racing across the landscape to find shelter.

Gramps stopped for a minute, "Where can dat boy be? I didn't see him anywhere round da cabin when I was thar. That poor boy, I bet he's scared stiff."

His head was throbbing from his injury and blood

was trickling down in his eyes again, but he kept going, "Timmy... boy where are ya? It's okay to come out now. I done proved ya is my real grandson."

Just then the wind made him unbalanced and he fell into a deep water-hole. He held Little Tom above his head with one hand and able to pull himself out with his other hand. He sat at the edge of the water for a few minutes trying to calm the frightened cat before getting up to continue to look for the lost boy. Now the sky was a charcoal black and the rain was building into a major storm.

"Oh Timmy, ya had it so bad and now ya can live wit me and I caint find ya. Where are ya boy?" The old man called out in tears.

The injured man seemed to be walking around in circles and decided to try to make it to the Indian village to get help in finding the boy. It seemed like it was taking forever but Gramps fighting the storm made it to the village, where he found everyone in panic. He didn't want to impose on anybody because they all were trying to prepare themselves for the brunt of the storm. He knew he could get help from the old Indian woman and went directly to the Chickee where he found Ghost Swamp

Flower huddling with Moses.

"You hurt!" The old woman said as she stood up to extend help to Mr. Sands.

"Naw I'm okay," he said.

"I am sure glad to find ya-all safe and sound but I cain't find Timmy... he's out thar somewhere in dat storm," he yelled at the top of his lungs almost in tears.

Moses stood up at once and said, "I'll go out thar an look fer him." He grabbed a length of rope and he ran out of the Indian shelter.

Gramps put the frightened cat in a basket and secured the lid so the cat would not run off and then taking the old Indian woman's hand said, "Ya come wit me and we will go look fer the boy too."

"Let me look at your wound," said the Indian.

"No woman, we ain't got time for that, sides it's just a scratch."

****

My throat was so sore from yelling that very little sound came from me now. What seemed like hours went by, I was being pelted by twigs, leaves and the abrasive rain. No matter what way I moved I couldn't cover my head to protect it all of the time. Suddenly a piece of a cypress limb flew by striking me on the head and arm and that is the last thing I remembered until I woke the next morning.

There was no lightning, no wind, and no awful sounds of anything. Dead calm. Except for the occasional gray puffy cloud the sky was a light blue color and I was alive. The palm that I was tied to was leaning at a forty-five degree angle and water was touching the bottom of my feet. I figured that I was about four feet up on the palm tree so I determined the water would be fairly deep where I was.

"Mos...!" I continued to cry, but no answer. Only the husky sound of my breathing and the beating of my heart were the sounds that I heard, nothing else... it was so quiet now. Such a change from just a few hours before.

I struggled to get my knife out to cut the ropes that held me and when I did to my surprise I fell backward into the water. I scrambled to get out of the water, and as I found a spot of dry land that was far enough from the water, I rested. The world looked so different and I had no idea where I was. I never saw so much destruction.

Whole stands of giant Cypress were bent over or flattened to the ground along with all of the palm trees that I could see for miles. There were still small fires burning and much smoke spiraling toward the sky, even with all the water that was everywhere.

Remembering what Gramps...I mean Mr. Sands... taught me about the sun and how to tell what time of day it was and what direction I was going in. I figured that it was around nine o'clock in the morning and I was facing south-east. That was about the direction of the cabin, so after trying to call out for Mr. Sands or Moses one more time and not hearing anything, I started for the cabin.

The old Indian woman was at the verge of collapse and Gramps was sickened with disappointment that they couldn't find Timmy. In the early morning light and with great reluctance, they turned back toward the Indian village. Arriving back at the village they sadly found almost total destruction. Their hopes were also shattered when they found that neither Moses nor the boy was there. But they thought that it was still possible that the albino found Timmy and they were both safe somewhere in the swamp.

"Was anyone or anything in spite of the great storm

alive in the vast swamp?" were the thoughts spinning about in my head. "As far as that goes... is anybody alive in the whole world?"

Stumbling around the desolate landscape I yielded to my weakened body and sat down on a overturned palm tree by the edge of a flooded area. Whole colonies of fire ants were clinging to leaves floating on the top of the water looking for places where they could eventually climb on dry land to reestablish new homes. Even now with all this death and destruction God showed his forgiveness and took pity on the lowly ant and saved them from oblivion. Again I was threatened with the cold emptiness inside that would not relieve me of the sadness around me.

There were no birds or small animals, only dead fish and the occasional carcass of a dead deer. The farther I walked the more devastation and death I saw. The complete destruction of the land by the hand of Mother Nature and I was truly humbled by what I saw. I saw flocks of buzzards feasting on whatever dead that was scattered about, not distinguishing between large or small. They were already picking the bones of deer, raccoons, bobcat and even a dead black bear. The buzzards were the only ones that were benefiting from all the death. Buzzards were impartial because they ate from any dead same as worms. Thank God I didn't see any people but I didn't know where anybody could be.

"Moses," I continued to shout out hoping that he was still going to come back for me, but he did not answer.

The pain in my body was agonizing and every step I took as I climbed over tangled thickets and downed trees was a struggle but some how by luck I found my way back to the cabin. How I don't know because the landscape was totally changed. Where there was land before, was just water now and where the water was before, was littered with so many trees and brush that nothing looked the same. The outside of the cabin was stripped bare, all the skins were gone, the tree stumps and where the fire pit was, was washed away.

I called out for Gramps, Moses, Jull or anybody, hoping there was someone in the cabin. No answer. Little Tom... where is he? I looked everywhere around the outside of the cabin for him and uncertain that I would find him in the same condition as the other animals.

Stepping into the cabin, the musty smell overtook me and I could see where the water moved everything around and there still was water standing in several spots. I set the table up along with the two chairs and was surprised to see the paintings were overwhelming bright and vivid as when I painted them. I called for Little Tom and looked everywhere for him, but no Little Tom. Looking under the cot I feared the worst that Little Tom had drowned and washed under the cot. No black cat, just a dead raccoon that was caught in the storm and perished inside the cabin.

My belly was growling so loud telling me to look for something to eat. I found a tin of biscuits washed into the corner along with a couple of oranges. It was so damp and cold in the cabin that I went outside and not finding a place to sit down, I decided to climb on top of the cabin. Once on top of the cabin I could see just how much destruction there really was. There was water everywhere with no signs of any life, animal or human, just some buzzards feasting on some unidentified swollen carcass. The puffy white clouds formed giant sand castles in the sky, and as they moved, it was like watching water moving in the surf. I stayed on the roof all day and slept there that night.

The next day the water had receded enough that I felt

I could try to find the Indian village and hopefully Mr. Sands with Little Tom safe and unharmed. Climbing down from the roof, I noticed a white-belly slithering at the edge of the cabin looking for a warm place to lay and heat his cold body. I saw no need for any more lose of life so I just eluded him and walked wide around him. I struggled through the land for what seemed like hours and finally stumbled on what I thought was the Indian village or at least what was left of the it. People where sorting through the debris to see what they could salvage and tending to their wounded. There were no structures left standing and I learned later that no people in the village were killed.

Chapter 24

"Timmy... thank God yur alive!" yelled Mr. Sands looking up with tears in his eyes and seeing me stumbling into the Indian village.

The old Indian woman and the man that I called Gramps was helping several Indians set up a Chickee, a form of an Indian hut made out of Palmetto thatch over a cypress log frame, so they could get the injured out of the sun. As soon as he saw me, Mr. Sands stopped what he was doing and ran to me. He picked me up and covered me with his strong arms and said, "God is truly great and He done brought ya safely back to me."

I clung to him for a long time while my tears mingled with his, we cried and laughed together.

"I thought fer sur ya was dead," he said. "

The Injun an me went out lookin fer ya and had to come back caus the old gal couldn't go no farther in the storm. We also sent the albino boy out to look fer ya too," he went on.

"Have ya seen him, boy?"

I stopped crying for a second and said, "Yes Moses found me. He tied me to a palm tree, and that is what saved me from being blown away in the storm. Where is he? I want to thank him and give him a hug for saving my life."

"He ain't back yet," The old man said, lowering me to the ground.

I looked at Gramps and noticed that he had a large cut on his forehead. "Your hurt, are you okay? How is Ghost Swamp Flower? And what about the two men I left you with? And most of all, where is Little Tom? Is he okay?" I went on and on until the old man had to stop me so he could get a word in and start answering some of the questions that I was throwing at him.

"Son... to start wit, Little Tom is fine. He is wit Jull. And she is fine too, just plum tuckered out. And bout them boys ya left me wit... well they ain't gona bother us anymore."

Oh no Gramps done them in! I was hoping not to hear that, and I braced for the bad news

The old man smiled a full-size grin and said, "I got some powerful good news to tell ya."

"What Gramps, what is it? How could there be any good news that could come out of all this destruction and death of wild life?" I thought wiping some tears from my eyes."

"That's just it, them boys ain't goin bother ya or me again because ya is really my grandson!"

I stood there looking at him, trying to figure out what he said and more important... what he meant.

He picked me up again and wrapped them big burly arms around me again and I thought he was going to squeeze my iners out of me.

He sounded all choked up when he said, "Did ya hear what I said? Ya is my real grandson by ya Ma's side. And I got the proof of it. Ya Pa married my daughter and I got a photo of them the day they got hitched at the church where we used ta live in Henderson Creek. I bout fell over when that Mr. Strum told me ya last name were Dalton, Timmy Dalton. That yu Pa's name were Hector and yu Ma's name were Grace... that were my little girls name, Grace! Don't ya see boy... ya is really my true grandson," He said so excited and happy.

My Grandpa told me after all we went through, *"Redemption is a funny thing... sometimes you have to go through hell to get to it!"*

I thought back when living in the shack at Buzzard Bay, I did remember seeing a photo of what Gramps was describing to me, but I was too stunned with what he just told me to grasp the great news.

Gramps stopped hugging me so tight and looked at me, "Did ya hear what I said, boy? Ya is my grandson and ya kin live wit from now on, and nobody is gona take ya from me."

Tears flowed by buckets and between them were met with cries of laughter. With everything that has happened to me in the past, all the bad, all the loss in my life, this great news all of a sudden came flooding over my body and drenched me with uncontrollable happiness. I buried my face into the old mans chest and continued to weep. I don't know how long I cried or how long Gramps held me but after awhile I began to laugh again. I doubled up laughing for a very long and wonderful time.

"Oh Gramps I am so happy and thankful to God for

saving my life and making this wonderful news come true." I said. "Now can I go tell Little Tom the great news?"

We walked back to the Chickee where Little Tom was coiled up in a basket. As soon as he saw me he jumped out of the basket and into my arms. Petting Little Tom, I walked over to Jull and greeted her and thanked her for looking for me and taking care of Little Tom. Then I explained how Mos found me and by tying me to a tree I was able to make it through the terrible storm.

She put her hand on my arm, looked deep into my eyes and asked, "Where Blue Eye Cat?"

That was the most words I ever heard her say, and I was very sad to tell her, "I don't know. After he tied me to the palm tree he left and I never saw him after that. He saved me and I owed him my life and I would be forever grateful to him."

She never said anything after that, just went back to attending a fire where she was fixing "boiled swamp cabbage" a food that was from the heart of the cabbage palm.

Gramps, and I could truly say that now, as we sat under one of the few trees that was still standing and ate the meal that the old Indian woman fixed for us and the rest of the Indian people.

"Have ya been to the cabin?" asked Gramps.

With a mouth full of food I answered, "Yes sir. There wasn't anything left on the outside and the inside was a real mess, but I think we can fix it up with a little hard work.

Gramps set his bowl down on a log and said, "Were the paintings that ya did still thar?"

"Yes sir. I put a little water on the wall and to my surprise it looked pretty good yet."

I stood up to go get another bowl of boiled swamp cabbage and said, "It might be hard going for us for a while but I think with God's help and care we will be okay. People in town might need help repairing their damaged homes and maybe we can make some money that way until the gators come back."

"Boy... we don't has to worry none, I been givin these Injuns silver dollars to save fer me for years. They had my permission to use what they needed to help care for them and the rest of the money they has buried in a iron chest in a sacred place here in the village."

Gramps went on to say that Jull told me the money

was safe and that the Indians used very little of the money over the years, so there was thousands of silver dollars in the chest.

"In a couple of days we will go to Rattlesnake Pass and see if'n we kin help dem poor souls there. We kin help dem without taken any pay fer it, if'n that is okay wit ya son? Maybe by then the albino boy will be back and he kin go wit us."

I thought to myself, I went into the swamp, lived through a great storm, and I have come out as a BIG GROWN UP MAN.

Chapter 25

Rattlesnake Pass was still in the general location where it had been but in name only. All the structures were damaged and some had only the foundation left. The whole town had been flooded so most all of the buildings except the ones that were on high ground, would have to be torn down and rebuilt. Gramps made good on his word to help the townspeople. After helping the Seminole Indians get back on their feet we went to Miami. There he bought three wagons loaded with food, clothing and hard to get supplies and gave everything to the people of Rattlesnake Pass and never asked anybody for a cent.

A few days before we went to Miami to buy the supplies, some Indians found the body of Blue Eyed Cat. His twisted body was found about a half mile from where I was tied to the tree. He saved my life and in return he gave up his life. I will forever be indebted to his memory. When the old Indian woman was told about Moses, she unrolled her hair, a Seminole custom to show a personal state of mourning. Then she went off to be alone and wept, that was the only time I ever saw any emotion from her.

Buzzard Bay did not come out of the storm nearly as good as Rattlesnake Pass. The town was totally destroyed but eventually in a period of time was rebuilt, bigger and better then before. The hardware store was for the most part gone, except for the front wall of the building where my fathers sign was still attached to the building. The same sign that I was permitted to paint the little bird in the upper corner.

Mr. Leon S. Boxer perished in the storm trying to help a neighbor and the hardware store was not rebuilt at least not in the same place and not until two years later. The town folk built a small museum on the location of Leon's store in dedication to the worst hurricane in history in that part of Florida.

Years later I made a trip to Buzzard Bay to look over the place where I lived with my Ma and Pa. The town had changed unexpectedly to my surprise. It looked like they rebuilt every building bigger and better than it was when I was a little boy. Most of the people were prosperous fishermen making a living taking tourists on fishing excursions and trying to see what boat could catch the biggest and the most tarpon in one day. There were many fancy fishing boats in the excellent new marina in the bay and just as many fine automobiles on the streets of Buzzard Bay. Several large buildings stretched throughout the downtown district along with a magnificent two-story schoolhouse where the old wooden one once stood.

I could not recognize the location where old Leon Boxer's hardware store was because in its place stood a small building with a sign on the front that read Buzzard Bay Historical Museum.

As I entered the front room of the museum I was greeted by a nice elderly lady sitting at a small desk located to the rear of the room.

"Hello young man, have you ever been in Buzzard Bay before?"

I took a quick glance around the room at the artifacts on display and said, "Yes ma'am, I lived here when I was a very young boy and I haven't been back for many years. The old town sure has changed a lot since I lived here and I hardly recognized it."

"This is the site where a hardware store once stood before the big hurricane of 1931 hit and wiped out most of the town. We built this museum in honor of Leon Boxer who lost his life in the storm. See this sign hanging in the show case, that was about all that was left of the store that was on this location. Do you remember the hardware store when you lived here?"

I walked over to the display and a blood-pumping rush washed over my body. I tried to catch my breath and forced a slight grunt sound out, "Uh- yes, I choked... yes," I tried to mumble the words. "I do remember the store," I stammered.

The wooden sign that my Pa painted with the name Boxer's Hardware Store on it was displayed in a glass case in honor of Mr. Boxer and for all of the rest of the people that died in the storm. That magnificent beautiful, wonderful sign!

I gently put my hand on the top of the cool glass case and leaned close to the display and I could swear I felt the affectionate presence of my father with me. There he was sitting on the porch and I was near by with the three little box turtles that got lose and caused the problem that we had to correct. Now here it is... the sign, the big beautiful magnificent sign. There was no damage to the sign and the paint was bright and vivid as if he painted it just yesterday. My eyes traveled upward to the spot that I painted the small bird and yes, it was right there where I painted it so many years ago. I started to shake, my skin turned a lighter shade and I started to sweat.

"Are you okay young man?"

"I... I... I," I just couldn't push the words out that I wanted to say.

"You better come over here and sit down and I will

get you a nice cold glass of water, maybe that's what you need."

Still looking at the sign I pulled myself away and walked backward as if in a trance to the chair and sat down. "I just got a little faint, it must be from the bright sun coming in the window. I should be okay in a few minutes," finally putting words to my blank face.

I drank the cool water in slow sips, still gazing at the sign and said, "Thank you for the water, I feel much better already."

Still trying to get my composure I let my eyes move about the room taking in more items that I could remember from my childhood. The school bell was found at the shore of the bay and also held a favorable place on display in the museum. That was all that was left of the school I first attended in the town of Buzzard Bay. I look intently at the shiny bell and thought I could hear its clang as it called us to school. In my mind I saw glimpses of Miss. Jones and my first girlfriend, Rose Bud Benton and even Samuel Brown the boy that took away my first love with just one ride on a pony. I could feel the jolt as I bounced in back of old Ned's school bus while he tried to hit every pot-hole he could find on our way to school.

Just then the front door opened and a man walked into the room.

"Hi Miss. Mary, I'll watch the museum while you go to lunch."

"Thank you Donny," she said while she straightened up her desk.

My trance was broken and I stood up and thanked the lady for the tour. Walking by the sizeable showcase that held the sign that my father painted, I whispered to him, good-by, and left the building and never looked back. That was the last time I was in Buzzard Bay.

If you ever visit Buzzard Bay for any reason, vacation, or fishing trip or whatever, stop by the museum. Go up to the case where my father's sign is on display and put your hand on the case and if you get a chill that goes up your arm over your shoulder and slithers down your spine, you will know this story is true. This will be the spirit of my farther saying, "Welcome to Buzzard Bay."

Weather forecasters for the year of the great hurricane said it was the most active year for storms in recorded history. The awful hurricane that I lived through changed my life forever. That year... I was pulled from childhood and was pushed unsteadily into adulthood without my permission.

Some say south Florida was changed dramatically by the Great Hurricane, but that is not true. The sun still rises in all its great splendor and sets with the most magnificent display of colors. The deer has come back, along with the bobcats and black bear. Even the large variety of beautiful tropical birds are again roosting in the trees that have grown back. This proves to me that left alone, God will put together what He has disturbed.

Afterward

The year is nineteen fifty-five and it's a wonderful time to be alive. The Great Depression has passed and it seems like everybody is making money.

I found out what it was like to fight in a war, the horrible World War II. I know now why my father was reluctant to talk about it, just as I am reluctant to talk about it. To this day it is hard for me to believe man could do the terrible things he did to his fellow man. It would take a lot of nails and a lot old wooden fences to be able to purge the souls of so many people that participated in that war.

Now they were all gone, Little Tom... Gramps... and the old Indian woman. And of course the albino Negro man that saved my life, Moses... Blue-Eyed-Cat.

With all that I had endured in my life, I still consider I have lived a charmed life. I live in a great country where on the most part we are free. Free to think what we want and in my trade, paint what I want to paint. It hasn't been easy, but life isn't... but all in all I can't complain. I have learned the hard way, when things go bad and you get knocked down, don't blame God or anybody else. Just get back on your feet and try life again. Odds are in your favor that you will make it the next time if you truly do try hard.

Today... after all these years and everything that has happened, I have come full circle. I receive great pleasure sitting with my seven year old son, the spitting image of a curly haired boy that I remember from the past. We are taking in all the colors of life at the edge of the Big Blue Cypress Swamp watching a great white heron. The eye-catching bird half-dozing on an old twisted cypress stump with the shadows and contrasts dancing with a gentle glow on the water, and I am describing to my son the method my father taught me of the best way to put this entire scene on canvas.

The Florida landscape now is being changed forever, not by God and nature but by greedy men that have drained the swamps and cut down the magnificent trees to build amusement parks, shopping centers and condos. What they didn't put a building on, they black topped over for roads and parking lots.

****

These last few lines are for the artist or want-to-be artist. So if you are not in this category... just don't read this. Now don't peek.

I debated for a long time whether to put this in the book or not because I didn't want to sound like I knew all there is to know about art or about life as far as that goes. I did not want to sound like I was preaching because that is the last thing I wanted to do.

I hear people say... "Oh you have so much talent, I can't even draw a straight line." Well, the truth is I can't draw a straight line either, but I have fun trying and that to me is all that counts. I have been able, over the years, to do what some people say is very good work, and believe me, I do appreciate all the praise that I get, after all I am human. But, now don't get me wrong, it is how I feel about something when I am finished with it that means the most to me. Did I catch you sneak a quick look at this part of the book?

What I am trying to say, it's not important if you are good at painting or not, it's how you think about what you do and how it makes you feel... or anything you do in life as far as that goes.

I want to say to all the people that have the great desire to create a painting, never give up. You never know you might be the next Rembrandt, Picasso or maybe even Grandma Moses. And when you reach the point that you finally call yourself an artist, you will have what I call an addiction... an unconscious appetite to put paint on something. I don't care if it is on canvas, wood, chairs or walls... and if you can make it even one day without painting or thinking about painting that you feel you will go nuts. Now you know you are hooked. Not that you are necessarily good or not because that really doesn't mean anything to you, like I already said, just that you can do what you are obsessed with... that's all that matters.

I am sure that you can find beauty in life everywhere you look, even in dead things... after all isn't a flower arrangement with dried dead flowers beautiful?

Now here comes the preaching, if you want to try

something artistic, do it. Don't say, "Well I don't have time or maybe I will some day, or I don't think I am good enough." That kind of talk just ain't going to cut it.

This is for all the people that just had to sneak a peek and read this part. All you husbands, fathers, mothers,

sisters, brothers or friends that know somebody that has the urge to draw or paint or anything in the art world... ENCOURAGE THEM! You will be better-off for it and I know they will be too.

Photo By Joyce Vebert

Dennis Vebert is a local artist that has lived in Florida for over 35 years. He is in his late 60's, is self taught, paints mainly in oil and acrylics, and has painted landscapes all his life. His style is realistic landscapes of Florida in which he tries to capture the exciting sunsets, exquisite sky and the stirring reflections in the water of the many lakes, rivers and swamps of the state. Recently he has engaged in a series of Aviation paintings that he finds very rewarding. He has written two children books and is the author of a very adult book "Mind Games", a story about life in the Unites States Marine Corps boot camp in 1961. Dennis Vebert lives with his wife in Central Florida and is now working on a murder mystery in between painting.

All of the paintings in this book can be ordered from the author, Dennis Vebert, in print form or in note cards. You can see these and many other paintings if you Google dennis-vebert.artistwebsites.com or go to www.fineartamerica.com or contact Dennis Vebert directly at 1025 Pennsylvania Avenue, St. Cloud, Florida. 34769 1-407-891-0277 or 1-407-892-6524. Or my personal email denjoy@embarqmail.com

Index of painting titles